Dad Had a Bad Day

Also by Ashton Politanoff

You'll Like It Here

***Headshot* meets John Cheever in this darkly funny, deeply moving portrait of what happens when a "sad dad" reconnects with a passion from his past.**

When Ned finds his old Slazenger tennis racquet buried in the garage, he unearths a part of his former self. Having recently lost his job, his sole duty is to watch over their six-year-old son while his wife works. On a whim—and without his wife's knowledge—Ned joins his childhood tennis club with a secret credit card, where he finds life outside the realm of "sad dad" domesticity. He becomes the captain of a local men's rec league team, reconnects with his old hitting partner and former tennis prodigy, Roland, and commits his whole sad self to building a winning team. But when Roland disappears, Ned's search for his friend threatens to consume the path to glory, the relationship with his son, his marriage, and his mind. A meditation on fathers and sons, male friendship, and the psychic pressures of an individual sport, Politanoff's novel sits beautifully alongside the dark comedy of Iris Murdoch and the masculine angst of John Cheever, with a style all its own. Funny, poignant, and deeply relatable, *Dad Had a Bad Day* explores our desire for structure, the emotional limits of domestic life, and the unbelievably potent, powerful, intoxicating feeling of winning.

Author photo by: Dui Jarrod

About the Author

ASHTON POLITANOFF is a frequent contributor to *Noon.* His writing has also appeared in *Southwest Review, Conjunctions, NY Tyrant, Egress,* and elsewhere. He is a former division I tennis player and his childhood coach was Robert Lansdorp, who is credited with coaching Pete Sampras, Tracy Austin, and Maria Sharapova. Politanoff's first novel, *You'll Like It Here* was published by Dalkey Archive. He is an English professor at Cypress College.

Dad Had a Bad Day

• • •

A Novel

Ashton Politanoff

Astra House ∧ New York

Copyright © 2026 by Ashton Politanoff
All rights reserved. Copying or digitizing this book for storage, display, or distribution in any other medium is strictly prohibited.
For information about permission to reproduce selections from this book, please contact permissions@astrahouse.com.
This is a work of fiction. Names, characters, places, and incidents are products of the author's imagination or are used fictitiously. Any resemblance to actual events, locales, or persons, living or dead, is entirely coincidental.
Astra House
A Division of Astra Publishing House
astrahouse.com
Printed in the United States of America

Library of Congress Cataloging-in-Publication Data

Names: Politanoff, Ashton author
Title: Dad had a bad day : a novel / Ashton Politanoff.
Description: First edition. | New York : Astra House, 2026. | Summary: "Headshot meets John Cheever in this darkly funny, deeply moving portrait of what happens when a "sad dad" reconnects with a passion from his past"— Provided by publisher.
Identifiers: LCCN 2025044247 | ISBN 9781662603433 paperback | ISBN 9781662603440 epub
Subjects: LCGFT: Fiction | Novels
Classification: LCC PS3616.O56754 D33 2026
LC record available at https://lccn.loc.gov/2025044247

First edition
10 9 8 7 6 5 4 3 2 1

Design by Alissa Theodor
The text is set in Warnock Pro.
The titles are set in Futura LT Pro.

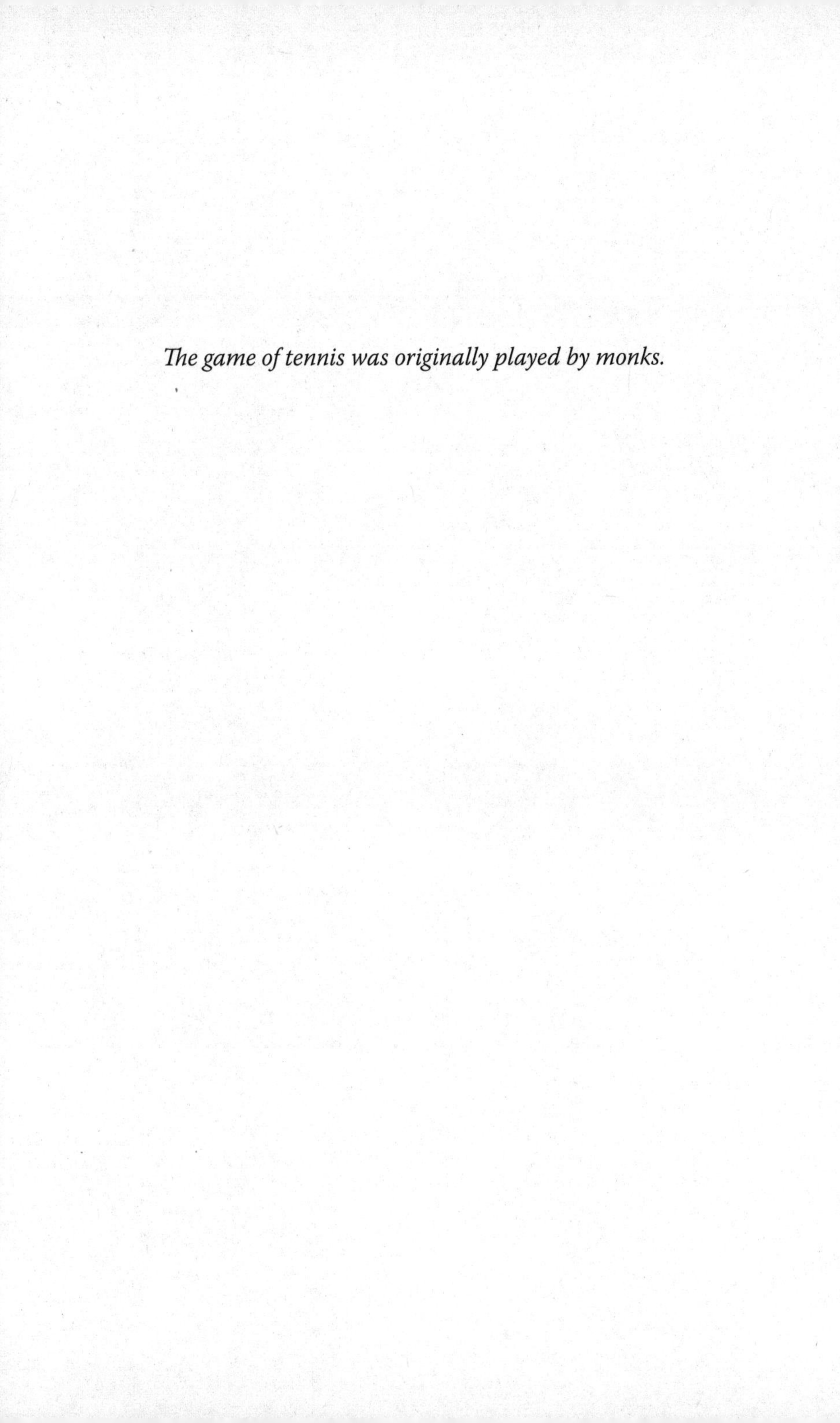

The game of tennis was originally played by monks.

Dad Had a Bad Day

Dear Loraine,

I am trying to find my purpose.

• • •

My wife was still at work. My son didn't want to go to the park, but I needed to get outside. He had a fever, so I gave him a glass full of ice cubes and told him to suck on them during the drive. His school wouldn't take him back until the fever was gone. I drove in a direction until we found a park. The park was one we hadn't been to. The grass around the playground was tall, uncut, and I followed him down the concrete path. The sky was orange, with only a few clouds as the sun set in the distance. A girl was on the swings. She was self-sufficient, tucking her legs behind her and straightening them forward, building momentum. My son was not self-sufficient. He still needed me to push him. The swing the girl was on was silent on the way up, but it sounded like a bird's chirp on the way down. It was rusty. The girl was alone. My son climbed some steps leading to a slide, and I took a seat on a wooden bench with chipped green paint. Directly across from me, behind the playground were two tennis courts. They looked slick and worn from use, and the nets sagged down the middle. On one side of the nearest court was a young man, a towhead, my guess would be eighteen, and on the other side was an older man, presumably his father. The young man took his racquet back for a forehand with a quick shoulder turn, all the time in the world, his feet making tiny little squeaks as he moved. He sent the yellow ball in a clean arc deep to the other side of the court. The father with the sport sunglasses was competent. The rally continued. The constant percussion of the ball being struck with trained perfection by the young man sent a vibration through me. I found myself walking toward the fence, the sound of the ball, the flick of the wrist, feet stepping forward like daggers then tumbling back like leaves, the ball hailing and then collapsing missile-like onto the hard court. Then, I heard a cry behind me. It was my son.

I put a Band-Aid on his knee in the bathroom and then turned on the TV. In the kitchen, I peeled the skin of a pear with a potato peeler. I sliced it with a large knife.

I want a peach, he said when I handed him the small rectangular Tupperware holding the fruit.

We don't have any peaches in this house, I said, walking away.

Where are you going, Dad?

To the garage.

Why?

I'm looking for something.

But I'm scared, he said to me.

Be brave, I said. I held out his blue eiderdown, the one he would disappear under.

We didn't keep a car in the garage. There was a dining table with broken legs, toys my son had outgrown, electronics that no longer worked. I found my old Slazenger racquet somewhere in the back. The overgrip was denim blue, faded and feathered. It felt soft and innocent in my hands. I heard my son calling me. I squeezed it hard. I started swinging, cutting the still air in the garage—*whoosh!* Forehand, backhand, forehand, backhand. My son. I kept swinging.

This way, I said, guiding with a flat hand. I could feel his bony shoulder blade under his T-shirt. I put on his backpack for him at the gate of the school. Have a great day.

Through the chain-link fence, I watched him walk to his classroom.

My son is blond, blue eyed, fair skinned. I have brown hair, light brown eyes, and I could be described as swarthy. My wife, she is blonde and green eyed, and although she tans easily, she looks Irish. Sometimes people ask me if my son is my son when I'm with him alone. When I tell them yes, they ask me again as if I've misunderstood the question. Don't they see his chin? my wife says to me. He has your chin, she tells me.

I got back in the car. I had an appointment.

At the entrance of the club, the fountain spat limply. Inside, behind the front desk sat a young woman with a waterfall of shiny black hair. She was wearing a forest-green crewneck sweatshirt with *Wind & Sea Tennis Club* printed on it.

Good morning, she said. How can I help you?

There were columns on either side of the desk, and a large bowl of flowers behind her. The flowers were stiff, fake. As soon as the name Ken left my lips, a man appeared from behind one of the columns as if he was waiting for me. He was tall and thin and red from the sun, and he had thinning brown hair. I noticed the white door of the side office next to the front desk. The door blended in with the wall, and even the knob was painted white, a detail I found tacky. They were trying to hide this office. He shook my hand firmly with a sweaty grip. If I had the opportunity, I would have washed my hands. He had his other arm in a sling. I asked him what happened. Elbow surgery he said. Had he had a black eye, I would have been suspicious of this answer.

Ken led the way. We weaved around the twenty-two courts and the groomed grounds. There was a gym, a lap pool, a kiddie pool. There was a bar and lounge, locker rooms with sauna and steam. There was the pro shop where racquets were strung. There was a balcony with seating that overlooked the club, a gazebo for weddings. In fact, not much had changed.

When's the last time you played tennis? he asked by the jacuzzi. The water had a green hue to it.

Fourteen years, I said.

Back in his office, Ken took a bite of his long john donut, wrote some numbers on a legal pad, and then ripped out the sheet. The yellow custard inside the long john oozed out onto a white napkin. I folded the piece of paper into my pocket and told him I'd let him know.

On the way out, I had to use the bathroom. The urinals were wall-mounted higher than usual. They made me feel like a small man.

For a time, the club was under a shroud. There were some incidences of disappearances, and the first involved a love triangle with a former tennis star—Larry Schiffer. His wife was said to be having an affair with their family doctor, also a member of the club. Larry went missing, and a shallow grave was found at the Schiffer home only to reveal the bones of a dead dog.

The second incident involved the club stringer—a man obsessed with the feel of natural gut. A few members had disappeared—a teacher, a minister who liked to swim early in the mornings, and the owner of several local knitting mills. Their remains were later found in drums of acid in the garage of the stringer's home.

You see, the stringer was convinced that natural gut from a human rather than an animal would have optimal performance in a racquet.

It's been said that he strung one of Ivan Lendl's racquets, the one he won Wimbledon with, with this very set of strings.

When I picked up my son from the after-school program, the light was dying in the west and a sheet of dark clouds was encroaching from the east. The field and playground looked doomed in the strange glow. It looked like the end of something. My son's fingernails were long and caked underneath with dirt. They needed cleaning. They needed cutting. I strapped him into his seat and put the car in reverse.

I really want a toy, Dad, he said.

Dad, he said.

What.

Can we get a toy from Target?

No.

You promised.

I didn't answer. A few heavy drops of rain splattered against the windshield, thudded against the roof. My son, he began to cry.

There was a parking structure underneath the Target, but I parked outside.

I'm getting wet, Dad, he said outside the car. I made a roof over his forehead with my hand.

Inside, my son led the way. The floors looked like a hospital. I followed him to the toy section and we started in the Lego aisle. He pointed at some things.

Too expensive, I said.

Next was the action-figure aisle and then the puzzle and board-game aisle. He didn't point at anything this time. We returned to the Legos. I told him the budget was twenty dollars.

Dad, this Target doesn't have anything I like. Can we go to another Target?

The other Target is closed.

No it isn't.

Yes it is, I said.

You're lying.

They're remodeling.

I want to go to another Target!

No.

My son, he sat on the ground. He began to whimper, and a store employee, a woman in a Target team shirt appeared.

Can I help you? Is everything okay?

Yes, we're fine, I said. Thank you—but the woman, she remained. She took a few lingering steps, looking at me, looking at my son, looking at me again.

I'll pretend you're not my father again, my son whispered.

Don't you dare.

Then get me that! he said pointing at a Lego box, a shipwreck and island set that cost $79.99.

I shook my head.

I want my mom and dad!

Stop it right now.

I glanced down the aisle, and the woman was still there. I had no choice but to pick him up.

Put me down! You're not my real dad! I draped him over my shoulder and headed for the exit. The employee, she was on her walkie-talkie. She said something I couldn't make out as she trailed behind, and there were lines of people in the front with baskets and carts waiting to checkout. The sky was black outside. My son was screaming.

It wasn't until I made a right onto Artesia that I noticed the cop car behind me. I told my son to calm down. I told him the police were here.

You're going to jail! he said. The squad car strobed its lights, let out its little tune, and I did as I was commanded.

The rain was coming down now, and I turned off the windshield wiper. The windshield bled red from the stoplight, the massage parlor neon, and I lowered my window where I met the eye of a flashlight.

Driver's license and registration please.

I reached into the glovebox and handed over the documents including a copy of my son's passport.

I assume you think this is an attempted kidnapping? The officer didn't respond.

This has happened before, I added. It's his way of bribing me to get what he wants. My wife and I are working on it.

The officer was blond and blue eyed. He could have been the father.

I don't want my dad to go to jail.

The officer studied my license, then me, then my son. A big truck rushed past, and I could feel its draft.

When we got home, all the lights were off, the house empty. From the freezer I removed a package of mac 'n' cheese. I punctured the plastic cover several times with the tip of a small knife before zapping the whole thing in the microwave.

First, they cut my hours in half, then they put me on straight commission. Then I was 1099'd, furloughed, idled, and finally laid off. The bills, they wouldn't stop coming in. My wife was a project manager. When there wasn't work, she wouldn't work, but we didn't know when she wouldn't have work. So when she came home last night and said that we needed to save, I agreed. Daddy daycare it is, I said.

The next morning, I called the club. I asked for Ken.

Ken, I said. Do you have childcare at your club?

Affirmative, he said. He gave me their morning and evening hours, and the price was included in the monthly membership should I want to put my son on my plan—it would be slightly more expensive.

I hadn't done anything yet. No paperwork was signed, no credit card given. The thing of it was, I needed my own separate card from my wife's account. Budget is budget, and I didn't want to be separated from my wife. But I also needed to take care of myself.

I found the most recent credit card offer addressed to me specifically in the trash. I slapped it free of some discarded and dry jasmine rice. I called the number and signed up. Then, I called Ken back.

Did I want to add anyone else to the membership, a spouse for example?

No, I said.

Part of the membership paperwork, in addition to a clearer breakdown of fees—initiation fee, first month / last month, towel fee, monthly mandatory food charge—and other legalese, was a code of ethics:

It is deemed unbecoming if any member engages in (a) a reckless display of anger, (b) caustic, unwelcoming language, (c) obscene gestures, (d) racquet or ball abuse, (e) emission of any bodily fluids outside of a bathroom stall or shower, (f) bathing in the pool with toiletries, (g) voluntary flatulence in the steam room or sauna, (h) physical harm to club members or property.

I could see Court 5 from the slightly elevated jacuzzi. I had a jet on my right trapezius when I saw the father and son walk together on court. The father walked ahead of the son in silence, and they put their bags down on opposite sides of the bench. The father retrieved a jump rope from his bag. The father wore a red bandana. He skipped rope in one of the alleys of the court while the son jogged a lap. The son jogged one more lap, and the father stopped jumping once his son stopped running. The father popped a fresh can of Dunlop balls, put two in his pocket and bounced the third with his racquet. They met on opposite sides of the court, warmed up with some mini-tennis starting from the service line, followed by rallies from the baseline, then each alternating volleys and overheads, followed by serves. Then, the father spun his racquet, the son pointed up, the correct call was down, and the father elected to serve, all this done through gesture. The son had jet-black hair spiked up with gel. The father, I could see the veins in his neck, his face bright red and straining as he tried to muscle a serve into the service box, swinging with the full meaning of his small body as he tossed the ball into the air, only to strike it straight into the net. The son proceeded to pounce on his pop-up second serve and break his father at love. Upon losing his serve, the father smacked a ball to the other side of the court. The son had no reaction. As they were switching sides at 1–0, the father unzipped a smaller pocket of his tennis bag and procured two white wrist sweatbands and slipped them on. Once on the other side of the court, ready to receive, the father tugged his red shorts up his thighs as he squatted. The father was climbing up a mountain while the son was going for a walk. Over the next fifteen minutes, the father shattered one racquet, sent two balls over the fence into the parking lot of a medical plaza (requiring him to open a new can), yelled *fuck you* presumably to himself, removed his bandana and replaced it with a hat, and ultimately stormed off the court without waiting for his son. His son, I could tell, enjoyed beating his father.

Dear Loraine,

I don't know if you know that I know, but we were at the park last week, the three of us, when I heard you speak to the other man. He was standing at the foot of the climbable rocket ship. Let me be clear. There were many moms and dads there, but you only spoke to one briefly in passing, a man with a shaved head mind you. You complimented his children when you said, "You make such beautiful children," but you were also complimenting him. The man had olive skin and dark hair—one could tell even though he had a shaved head because his eyebrows were still intact—and his young sons, his two boys, had the beginnings of his strong straight nose, his complexion, his hair color. When you said, "You make such beautiful children," it felt like a compliment to his semen. And I found that deeply offensive.

Yours,
Your Husband.

There was a new generation of members at the club. These were the kind of members that would arrive at the pool around 11 A.M. on a weekend, looking for chairs. The kind of members that would wait for the snack stand to open at 11:30 A.M. so they could order a hot dog, a tuna melt. They came with their kids, and the dads would keep their T-shirts on unless they entered the water. The moms would come with a book as if their time would be leisurely, but the books were never cracked. These members didn't play tennis. They didn't know the rich history of the club. They didn't even grow up here. They all moved here. The pool was full of bodies by noon, and the jacuzzi was so crowded that the water lapped over the edges.

I took my son into the men's locker room where there was another jacuzzi—empty.

This is nice, Dad, he said, touching my arm, as we sunk in and sat, a soft jet against each of our backs.

Then we removed our wet trunks, and I placed them in the hole of the water extractor, pressing the lid down until it stopped jittering. I plucked a couple plastic swimsuit bags from the roll.

We ordered our lunch from the bar. There was free popcorn from the popcorn machine, self-serve. We had a television to watch.

My son, he was happy, and so was I.

After placing my son in the childcare, I picked up my restrung racquet from the pro shop, charging everything to the card. The front desk gave me a key to a shed on Court 9 that contained a ball machine and baskets of pressureless balls. The shed was cobwebbed. I plugged in the machine and poured the basket of balls into it. I pressed the ON switch and heard it stir for a while. Then, a ball exploded out of its mouth to the other side, slapping the green screen of the back fence. I dialed down the speed and calibrated the other settings until the balls spat appropriately before running to the other side. My timing was off, and my legs weren't there, but it felt good to strike the ball again. I focused on forehands, trying to time my split step with the machine's release. Then, I ran around my forehand and hit some one-handers until the thing jammed up. A ball was stuck somewhere near the mouth, lodged in the gears. When I couldn't fix it, I unplugged it from the socket underneath a light pole and hit a few serves.

The shadow of a still palm tree slowly stretched and lengthened across the court, and I sat in the shade of the cabana bench. I sipped from a cool blue Gatorade.

At the front desk, I gave back the shed keys and asked for a couple of towels. I reported the problem when Ken appeared.

How's it going?

Great! I'm off to the steam room.

Ken pulled me aside, spoke low.

Rupert might be in there, he said.

Who's Rupert?

He's totally harmless, a total sweetie, but he does tend to scream at times. It is part of his condition. We haven't had any incidents with him lately, and if you notice anything, please report to me immediately. I can let his mother know.

So he's a child?

He's forty-five years old.

What does he look like?
You'll notice him right away.

The steam room was right next to the sauna in the back of the men's locker room next to the showers. I used a day locker to store my shoes and clothes, but I kept my shorts on. I walked barefoot to the steam room where I grabbed the metal handle. The door was glass, but it was dark and cloudy inside. There was a light switch that didn't work. I pulled open the door and my feet met the warm wet ground. Some of the steam rushed out as I went in, and immediately I saw a figure, a man with curls of hair that covered his ears, standing statuesque. He was in profile in relation to me, and his neck turned slowly to where his big, bright, unflinching eyes met mine, his mouth a straight flat line of severity. He looked like a powerlifter, an animal I was passing in the wild, and I found a seat on one of the tall steps away from him, but close enough to the door just in case. He grunted a little, poured some water on his back from a plastic water bottle and rotated his neck clockwise and counterclockwise. He repeated this action over and over again, and as my eyes adjusted, I observed that the man was completely naked from head to toe with his back toward me. Minutes went by before I noticed my irregular breathing, the heat and steam almost becoming suffocating. I would need to get out soon.

You're back, a voice said from the depths, somewhere on the other side of the steam room. This voice did not belong to Rupert, and as if to make this clear, Rupert looked at me sidelong, and then suddenly left. I heard the stuck wooden door of the sauna opened forcefully, Rupert's next stop.

Who's there? I said.

The champion is back.

Do I know you?

You probably don't remember me, but I remember you.

My body was slick, my shorts soaked. I could barely breath. I was ready to leave.

When did you join again?

Last week, I said.

I saw you hitting earlier. You're rusty, but you'll get it back quick.

I'm just playing for fun.

You can't just play for fun once you've tasted glory, the kind that you've had. You know who else is back?

My head started to feel heavy, like my neck could barely carry it.

Who?

Roland.

I stood up. I felt faint. I reached for a wall.

You remember Roland, don't you?

I kept my hand on the wall as I walked toward the door.

Nice talking to you, I said.

See you soon, the voice said.

The locker-room floor was carpeted green, and the walls were painted white. A panel of mahogany-framed photographs lined one portion of the wall, and I found Roland's picture there. The trophy he held at his waist was a large silver bowl filled with oranges, and his smile didn't show any teeth. The victory was expected. The next picture on the wall was mine. I was fifteen and the trophy I held was more of a plaque, barely larger than the palm of my hand. I held it above my head like it was Wimbledon.

Roland had a mother and a father and a sister, and the whole family joined the club a little after mine, when I was nine. Roland was older than me by a few years, but his sister was my age. Roland was the older brother.

When I first saw him on the court, he was playing a practice match. He had a beautiful one-hander—the way he took the racquet back before releasing reminded me of an archer. There was no awkwardness in his movements. He moved with grace and power. He'd go for the line, for the winner, and if he missed it, he moved on. There was an intensity about him, a quiet confidence, and he made little grunts with each shot. He walked with his shoulders back. He didn't rush between points, but he didn't move slowly either. He moved with purpose. Everything he did was with purpose.

I had the feeling that I was in the presence of future greatness.

In the middle of the night, I woke up to find my wife next to me. The long tube of the sleep apnea machine was connected to her face. She must have gotten in late. Her head rested in the valley of her cervical pillow—the width of it and the rise on either side created a mountain between us. I had a stiffy, but she was impossible to snuggle against. I rolled some earplugs into my ears and went back to sleep.

I remember when we first met—a philosophy class. Naturally, I sat in the back. I didn't notice her for almost the whole semester until the day I overslept and showed up thirty minutes late. There was only one seat left—right next to her. We were paired up for an activity that took up the rest of class time, and after class while I lingered and packed slowly, she offered me her notes for the lecture I had missed. I asked her instead if she wanted to grab breakfast in the cafeteria.

The cafeteria was nearly empty and we took a table by the window overlooking the grounds. It was a nice college, a private college. The floor was marbled and so was the table.

She looked at me directly. She wore makeup but it was faint, natural, and her hair was down. She had removed her sweater before we sat down, and now I looked at her across from me in a plain white tee. The neckline was drooped, and she wore a necklace with a pendant, a family heirloom I'd find out much later. In front of her was a cup of coffee, a little cream, and in front of me was a tall glass of orange juice.

How do you afford this place? I asked.

She asked me the same.

I told her about the partial scholarship I was on. I told her about the loans.

Loans, she said. Yes.

We had that in common.

I felt older than we were in that moment together.

I met her that Friday at the same table in the cafeteria, empty as the last time. We had our textbooks open before us, and I watched her loop letters with her colored gel pens. We were there to study, but I mainly watched her—the arc of her ear with a lock of hair nestled behind it, the line of her neck bent thoughtfully forward, the faint short blonde hairs on it.

Afterward, we went on a mission to find the professor's office together. I pretended that I wanted to see if he had office hours. Maybe she was pretending too. The halls were narrow, empty, and all the sliding doors with frosted glass were closed, locked. No professors were there. Our bare arms touched as she bumped into me. She did that more than once. Had I been a little braver, I would have reached out and grabbed her wrist until she looked at me. I would have kissed her.

Then the semester ended and it was summer, and I didn't see her again until the fall. She was out on the grass in front of the dorms throwing square sandbags, playing cornhole. She was barefooted in jean shorts. She looked happy. Next to her was another man in a sleeveless T-shirt, and they were tossing sandbags together, playing another couple. She saw me, smiled, waved.

And that was it. That was that.

I shouldered my heavy bag full of racquets to the practice courts, their laughter drifting behind me like distant birdsong.

Years later, I saw her again at a bar where the DJ played top-fifty cuts at a higher speed. We were in our late twenties at this point. I had quit tennis. I hadn't gone pro. We were working professionals now. Clock in, clock out. It was a weekend. I hardly recognized her at first. She wore more makeup, and I bought us some drinks. Within an hour we were on the dance floor making out, our friend groups nicely intertwined.

Whatever happened to you? she asked me later that night over a slice of greasy pepperoni pizza, and I didn't tell her. I didn't tell her what happened, about the team, about the coach. I didn't tell her about the fight, about my shoulder.

We moved in together a year later, engaged the following, then married. She became pregnant with our son, Frederick, in our second year of marriage.

We were different people now.

At the front desk, I asked if Roland was playing.

Yes, the young man in wire frame glasses responded. He's on Court 14.

Who's Roland? my son asked.

Just someone I used to know, I said.

I deposited my son in the toy room with Trina with a Ziploc bag of green pea snaps and a fruit punch before I made my way to Court 14. I walked beside the Japanese Boxwood and Worcester Gold shrubs before arriving at the backcourts. Court 14 was hidden behind a row of rose of Sharon, but I found an opening to view the court near the latched gate behind the baseline. On the near end was a boxy-looking fella with a two-hander. He slapped and hit a flat ball. They were mid rally, and on the far end was a tall figure in a long-sleeve white UV shirt that reflected the sun and blinded me. Hooked around his ears was a UV face mask that draped all the way down to his neck, and he also donned a cap. All I could see were his eyes.

His strokes were loopier, more precise, and he moved lightly and efficiently around the court, eventually slicing a ball and coming into the net for a stab volley that barely trickled over. He leaned over the net and pushed the ball to his opponent, stood straight up, and looked at me standing there. I raised my hand in greeting and he raised his hand back, but then I heard my name.

Ned, please come to childcare. Ned, please come to childcare, the PA system repeated.

He needs to use the restroom, Trina said, when I arrived.

I gotta poop, Dad.

You're a big boy. Can't you go by yourself?

He needs to be escorted by an adult, Trina said.

I let that fall.

We don't do the escorting, she added.

I marched my son over to the private unisex bathroom by the pool and locked the door behind us.

By the time his business was done, Roland was gone.

The next day though, I hit with him—Roland. I deposited my son and headed to the cardio center for twenty minutes of elliptical when I saw him, standing courtside, his racquets flat on a table.

Want to hit some balls? he asked me. His face was covered, but I recognized his voice.

Let me grab my stuff from the car, I said.

When I returned, he was already on a court within view, standing at the baseline, waiting for me.

We hit for twenty minutes. He hit a hard, penetrating ball concealed by relaxed strokes and minimal movement. He was gifted. He was an artist. His one-hander was more free-flowing than mine. He could disguise it—a slice, a dropshot, a drive.

I'm good if you're good, he said after twenty minutes, but I wasn't sure what he meant, if he wanted to play some games, a set, do some drills, take a break, so I said, Sure. Then, he walked over to the bench and took a seat. I sat down next to him.

I could have asked about his family, but I didn't. He kept his mask on.

You still got it, man, I said to him. He looked down. I could tell he was smiling by the way his eyes narrowed.

You still hit a good ball, too.

Where are you working these days? I said.

I'm at the FedEx off Franklin. It's mellow.

Nice, I said. You work every day?

When they need me, he said.

He said, Ever go down to the port?

Uh-uh, I said.

I get on that half-day boat there sometimes, the one that launches near the bridge. Caught some halibut yesterday. Gonna grill it tonight. You should come with me sometime.

Okay, I said. Sure, I said.

The fish, it excited him, I could tell.

Well, good seeing you, he said. Let's hit again, and before I could answer, he was off. I stretched out my hand, but he didn't see it in time.

I sat there, watched him walk away.

Roland, my old friend. My childhood friend.

He still hit a big ball.

We were ball boys together at the Virginia Slims, a professional women's tournament in the town over. We were assigned the same court in the early rounds, and in the heat of the second set, one of the players hit a ball into the net, on my side of the court. I sprinted up from the padded towel my knees were resting on and I decided to throw the ball across the court to the ball girl behind the baseline. I was trying to be fast. I was trying to be efficient. I missed the ball girl and hit one of the players right in the center of the back. Her shoulders scrunched up and she turned around and yelled at me in Dutch. Roland was right there on other side of the net, watching, in ready position for the next point, the next retrievable ball, like a track star. That was the first time I made him laugh. We couldn't control ourselves. Our supervisor saw our giggles and the umpire excused us both from the court. We became friends after that.

There was a flyer attached to a corkboard by a yellow pin, flapping in the wind: SUMMER LEAGUE, CAPTAINS NEEDED. There was an email address and a website.

Dear Loraine,

I think I found what I'm looking for.

There was one former member I remember. Henry. He would enter the club on work calls with his Motorola sandwiched between his cheek and shoulder. He scratched his crotch freely. He had strong calves and thighs and he often wore ankle socks and five-inch shorts to show them off, tan and shaved. He chewed and spat Red Man on court and he liked to serve out wide and come to net. It is said that his father was a hunter, a fighter, a sports fisherman, a real adventurer, and he himself was 100-percent Irish. He once grabbed another member by the balls and sent him a box of chocolates as an apology for doing so. He is no longer a member of the club.

Roland used to hit with the old red Head Prestige, the one Ivanišević played with. He was rangy, even at thirteen. Strong. He could slice. He could volley. He was all court. He was calm. I'd show up late to my lessons because I'd rather watch Roland play than play myself. I watched him beat full-grown men when he was still a boy. They'd break their racquets. They'd scream obscenities. They'd give him bad line calls, swat the balls away from him in frustration in between points. They'd change the score in their favor. It didn't matter. None of it did. Roland had the same calm about him no matter what. He had a golden glow around him. He'd always win. He was the best.

Now you know we can't tell Mom about the club, right? I looked at my son in the rearview mirror.

Why?

Because.

Because why?

It doesn't matter why. Just listen to me.

Well, then I want a new present from Target every day.

Once a month.

No.

Once a week.

Fine. But I want one today.

We can order one on Amazon.

Fine.

When we got home, I set up the TV and told him I'd get him a snack while he sat on the couch with a pillow behind his head.

I want gummies, he yelled from the living room.

We're all out of gummies, I said from the kitchen with my face in the pantry. I was staring at the bag of gummies, a medley of them. There was a fistful left. I reached in the bag, put them all in my mouth, and bit down—hard.

My wife referred to the schedule in our shared calendar, the one I never checked. She referred to it being the last day of my son's school before summer as I carried her roller suitcase down the stairs for her. Her hair was parted down the middle. Her cheeks were rosy with makeup, and her eyes were a stark green with special thanks to her eyeliner. By the shoe rack, she slipped into a fine pair of green ankle boots that zipped up the sides. I could see her purple bra as she bent down.

Give Mommy a big hug, she said to our son. Her phone was ringing and pinging, a work call and a notification that her driver was here, all happening simultaneously.

I have to go potty, my son said—still using the word "potty." I have to poop, he said, and I wanted to kiss my wife, but she was walking toward the door, and my son was scared to go to the bathroom alone, so I needed to follow him.

I'll see you in a week, my wife said right before she answered the call and shut the front door. I heard her suitcase being rolled down the driveway.

In the bathroom, I opened the window as my son took a shit.

To Whom It May Concern,

I am interested in captaining a men's team for the summer league.

Best,
Ned

That is wonderful news, Ken said over the phone. I told him my plans.

This is what I'll do. When you come to the club later today, I will have a men's hit list for you at the front. I'll put a mark next to the names of players you may want to recruit.

I appreciate that.

My pleasure. It is an important position, the role of captain. We haven't had a *Wind & Sea* team for some time.

It is my honor.

I shaved with a straight razor and put on a short-sleeve linen shirt.

I drove to the club.

The front-desk girl with long painted nails handed me the hit list, a stapled document. There were names, ratings, and phone numbers. I saw tiny little stars in black ink next to last names I didn't recognize—Stout, Gamble, Bray, Farley, Sampson, Ratliff, Snider, Burris, Dale, Wayne. Then I saw Belter.

Belter, Roland.

When I had problems with my old man, I'd talk to Roland about it. We would be sitting on the bench during the changeover, and he wouldn't get up. He would listen and let the silence hang. He knew that was what I needed. Then he'd make me laugh.

Roland's father would take him out on the court every morning at 5 A.M., right when the club opened. There would be an employee unlocking the front glass doors, and Roland's father would be first in line with a big basket of balls, ready to go. His father was an engineer and a veteran. He built their family house with his own bare hands.

Roland's father never smiled.

The number I tried rang three times before going to voicemail. The voicemail box hadn't been setup yet, I was told. Seeing Roland at the club again was all I could hope for. The next three days, he wasn't there.

I could hear my wife's voice downstairs.

I was in front of the mirror. I had my sweat-wicking polo on, unbuttoned. I tried on an elastic headband. I took it off.

My wife's voice continued. I could hear the stress in it. Maybe she was on the phone with the bank. Maybe she was trying to get us a loan. Paying a bill. Car insurance or homeowner's. Consulting with our financial advisor.

One must put those worries aside and live a little. Focus on the present.

I had my objectives in order. I was a tennis player now—again. Who's to say there was no worth in that? Who's to say that money seeking was more important than sport?

My wife's voice—it was incessant. I found some earplugs in a drawer and rolled them into my ears. I resumed my stance in front of the mirror. I practiced a split step. I shadowed a forehand, a backhand. My gaze—it was strong, focused.

I could hear her prattle still. I felt a combination of pity and impatience.

I split-stepped again, lunged forward. I looked good now. My stomach was already tighter and flatter, my shoulders wide and laid back.

I was a winner.

You're a winner, I said in my head.

Then I said it aloud.

Did I believe it? Yes. Yes, I did.

Did she believe in me? I made a pact with myself that it didn't matter anymore.

I grabbed myself by the balls, looked up at the ceiling, and thanked the heavens for this wonderful package, this endowment.

I made my way down the stairs loudly, proudly. My wife, she was still on the phone, on the couch, laptop on her lap, smart phone sandwiched between her cheek and shoulder. Beside her was our son, Freddie.

I filled up my water bottle slowly, methodically at the fridge's filtered waterspout. I grabbed my jingling keys from the china key bowl and opened the front door.

I closed it behind me.

I did not look back.

The marriage was a case of jealousy, malice, plain avarice. With gimlet glass on polished wood, Bray told me his full story. I sipped on a Saratoga and listened.

He lost his job due to cause in 2012. His wife was studying for her degree in business. He fell into a depression while responsible for the childcare of their three young children. His wife stopped showing up for her exit exams. He tried to coach her through it. She became violent—wooden ornaments were thrown at his head during the holidays, his face was smacked while driving 80 mph on the freeway, she took a paring knife to his pecker but stopped just short. He only punched walls. Fast-forward a couple years—they got through the toughest parts through couples therapy, a cocktail of medication, and a vacation to the Babuyan Islands—she was now an executive and he was also traveling for work. One night she texted him while he was on business that she hated him and she wished he was dead.

Then, she had a coworker that became a little too friendly. The coworker was married with kids, and one evening they attended the company holiday party. The resultant evening was filled with lingering looks and touches between his wife and her coworker. He tried to sleep on it but couldn't that night; the next morning he confronted her, but she denied all the accusations he had made. Two days later, her laptop was open with her email pulled up, and he played around with the keywords. He remembered his first name—Craig—and he also typed in the word "horny" and found nothing. He did find an invitation to a game night from Craig. She accepted the invitation via email. He cross-checked their joint family calendar for the dates and saw "work drinks" for a blocked-off period of time. Then, he overheard his executive wife talking to a friend and describing Craig as a handsome, calm man with a very nice future pension. He wrote an old-fashioned handwritten note to his wife about his findings and feelings, which she held underneath a lighter. It was a messy divorce.

He lived solely on ice cream sandwiches for two weeks. Tennis saved his life, he said.

I asked Phil Bray if he wanted to join my team. I told him my plans for captaining.

Count me in, he said.

Dear Loraine,

I am forming a kinship with these men.

I hired a personal trainer named Mason. He gave me a worksheet with a front and a back that we kept in a filing cabinet by the water fountain inside the gym—I had my own folder with my name on it. The front of the sheet was upper body, and the back was lower body. I used a golf pencil. We focused on the main muscle groups—back, chest, shoulders, biceps, triceps, quads, hamstrings, glutes, calves. I hired a tennis coach named Joachim, a Norwegian-Swede mix. He had me working on slapping rather than driving the ball. He told me to hit it like a penguin. I hired a masseuse named Vasanta. She worked on my neck muscles and underneath my armpits. I made smoothies at home with power greens, pitted dates, blueberries, almond milk, vanilla-flavored plant-based protein powder, and cacao nibs. I purchased some polos, some grommets, some string savers, head and lead tape, athletic boxer briefs, jock-itch cream, moisture-control sports socks, antifungal foot spray, callus and corn shaver, some tea-tree foot scrub. I purchased books with titles such as *Champion Mindset* and *Mental Toughness in Tennis.* I applied zinc oxide to the bridge of my nose. I stood in front of the mirror and repeated positive affirmations. I kept a journal. I charged everything to the secret credit card I kept behind my driver's license in my Montblanc wallet.

Inside the locker room, we showered next to each other, but in separate stalls. I could hear the young man whistling over the running water, and when the whistling was done, I knew he was finished. Still, I took my time. I soaped myself hard. The water, it was very hot.

I got out, and he was now by the sinks. He was backlit by a small window and naked, with one leg up on the marble counter, his balls and penis dangling. He was using a boar bristled hairbrush on his leg, starting from up high, on the inside. His leg hair was curled and finally groomed—it looked like bronze fleece.

We sat on tall stools at a high table on the balcony overlooking the grounds of the club. We could see every player on every court.

His name was Thiago.

I poured him another spicy margarita from the pitcher.

Now that he was in his two-button polo, none of his chestnut-colored chest hair even showed.

What followed was a story of great emotion. In short, the young man did not have a father. His eyes were wet and so were mine.

I asked him if he would like to join the team and without hesitation, he accepted my invitation.

We were scheduled to hit next Tuesday.

The swimmer wore a boxer-brief Speedo and a slip-on right knee sleeve. He had a nicely trimmed peppery mustache, the rest of his face shaved clean, and he wore a pair of neon-green reflective goggles. He got down in a sort of crouch, almost a runner's lunge, peering over the edge of the pool, his open lap lane, and all I could see was the top of his silvery head. He held this position for a good while. At first, it looked like he was stretching. After a minute, I thought he was praying. When I assumed the worst, that he had stroked out in this half-standing position—hey! I even called—he fell forward into the water making a big messy splash. I saw him breaststroke the entire length of the pool. He did not come up for air once.

In the wide racetrack mirror above the sinks, a man applied a lotion to his belly. The man had a towel wrapped around his waist, and he had no pubic hair as far as I could tell—the towel hung low. He applied the lotion to his belly with both hands and pumped more of the white cream into his palm from the blue bottle next to him. He massaged his belly like he was massaging dough. His belly—it looked like a pinched face.

Dear Loraine,

I have found a new species of men in these halls. These are men of ritual, discipline, and refinement. My hope is that over time their good habits will rub off on me.

Bray thinks he can hang with the young guns now.

He's become a cocky little fuck, hasn't he?

He finally got some pussy after his divorce is what happened.

Lost a few pounds, and he thinks he's Philippoussis.

I pulled my jeans up and kept my shirt off, and I walked around my aisle to theirs.

One of the men was sitting on a bench untying his shoes. The other was standing, still sopping from the courts. They were fresh off.

Let's give Bray some respect, I said. Especially in his absence.

The men, they looked at each other—the one sitting looked up and the one standing looked down. The one sitting was in a position of weakness. The one standing was in a position of strength.

Who the fuck are you? the one standing said.

You must not respect yourself to talk about someone else like that. If you respected yourself, you would respect Bray.

Well, maybe Bray doesn't respect us, okay, pal?

If you respected yourself, Bray might respect you. And even if Bray didn't respect you, and you respected yourself, his feelings about you wouldn't matter, now would they?

Buddy. Fuck off, okay? the one standing said. He looked down at the man sitting and laughed.

I am the captain, I said, taking a step forward. I stood straight and tall. I didn't lean forward or bend my neck.

I said, Bray is on my squad, and I don't like how you are speaking about one of my men.

Captain of what? the one sitting said.

The men's league team.

I let the official news sit in the air, and the men grew silent. They no longer looked at each other. I turned my back and returned to my aisle, where I applied some deodorant, put on the rest of my clothes, tied my shoes, zipped my bags, and left.

Those men, they didn't say anything more. They didn't say anything more because they wanted to be on my team.

The cabriolet was well polished. As it turned into the parking lot into a spot, the sun hit its ornament hood, blinding me. The man who drove it wore a herringbone newsboy cap. He had thick tufts of hair the color of oak that descended around his small tan ears. The man got out of the car, leaned in, and grabbed his tennis shoulder bag from the camel-leather backseat. He left the top down. The key ring dangled from his index finger as he spun and caught the keys repeatedly while he walked.

With my lamb-gut strings, I played the podiatrist on center. We agreed to play a set after the warm-up, and he peppered me with questions from across the net in between points.

Why did you quit tennis?

Or—

What does your wife do for work?

And—

Do you get along with your son?

How's the job hunt going?

So on.

I felt he was trying to distract me. We remained on serve until 4–4. A crowd of onlookers had accumulated—poolside, on the balcony outside the bar, faces in the gym window. There were claps and exclamations after long exchanges. I took deep breaths in through the nose and out through the mouth after each point. I stuck to my routine. I broke the podiatrist with a dropshot-lob combo to win the set.

After we shook hands, he asked how my feet were holding up, and if he could take a look. I removed my shoes and socks and sat reclined on the tall steps. The podiatrist sat sidesaddle. From his bag he removed a compact zip organizer with his tools. He scrubbed the bottom of my callused left foot with a foot grater. Then, he attached a disposable scalpel blade and punctured a friction blister on my right. He rubbed the wound with an infection-prevention wipe and applied an adhesive pad.

Keep an eye on this mallet toe, he said, and I thanked him.

On the drive home, someone was calling me. The car Bluetooth intercepted the call, and I pressed accept.

Ned?

Speaking, I said.

Ned, the club childcare is closing.

I could hear children in the background, a crash of plastic toys.

I checked my rearview and saw the booster seat in the back—empty.

Are you still at the club, Ned?

Yes, I am here, I said as I crossed a double yellow.

I'm on Court 5, I said. Be right there.

Dear Loraine,

Man's capacity for kindness and tenderness has revealed itself to me lately in glorious ways.

There's that feeling you get when things are on. You feel it when you lace your shoes—not too tight, not too loose. Just perfect. You feel it on the drive over—green-light city. Cruising. Your neck and shoulders feel relaxed, back aligned. You're handed not one but two warm towels at the front desk. The front desk is happy to see you. You step onto the court, and nothing feels tight. You skip some rope, jog a lap maybe. When you bend down to touch your toes, it doesn't feel strained. Then, in the warm-up, you feel like you have all the time in the world when you start at the short court. Your shoulders automatically turn and you bring your racquet back. Your racquet meets the ball in an effortless loop—you aren't gripping the racquet too hard. Your feet dance around and you have an abundance of energy. You're seeing the ball. It's as big as a volleyball. You can't miss. And when you move to the backcourt behind the baseline, the feeling continues. The court is your canvas and you're just painting, painting, painting, beautiful looping paint strokes back and forth. Slowly, you start to ratchet up the speed and you're still not missing. Mid-rally, you chip a ball and come in behind it, and your volleys are perfect. No backswing—just shoulder turn and a gentle jab. You're like Edberg up there. Rafter. McEnroe. Style and grace. The lobs come soon after and your overhead is flawless—120 mph with a spaghetti arm. Textbook. Classic. Then the serves. You progress at a measured pace. You warm up slow, but your placement is flawless. Lines and corners of the box—every single serve. Your ball toss is smooth—the ball doesn't rotate once. It goes straight up. Your knees are bending, your back is torquing, and your motion is constant. When the match finally begins, you're alert as a bird. You're as calm as a sloth. You're as fast as a pronghorn when your speed is tested. You're a master chef. Every ball you hit is a different spice—a slice, a drive, a heavy ball, a drop shot. You get the early lead and you don't let go. You almost feel badly about it. Your opponent is frustrated, frazzled, flummoxed. There have been some outbursts.

They're crumbling. You're speeding ahead. And soon, you're shaking their hand at the net. They're soaked and you're not. You could play for two more hours.

You could beat Roger Federer.

It was a birthday party with a bounce house in the driveway, but we were inside the real house. The flooring was marble in the living room. The other boy had my son in a headlock on the couch, but my son's head slipped out of the hold and, in turn, my son put the other boy's thigh in a leglock. They whispered to each other. The other boy shook his leg free and pinned my son face down into the cushion. With a fire-drill roll, my boy turned the tables on this other boy and got away and around. From behind, he forced the boy to sit down and held his neck between his legs. They were right near the edge.

The other father and I stood side-by-side. Out of the corner of my eye, I saw the other father take a sip of his beer.

So did I.

The woman with the navy-blue tennis visor and sleeveless dress sat under the striped canopy near the pro shop with a tennis racquet between her legs. She was trying to regrip her racquet when she looked up at me and smiled.

Are you good at this? she asked me. I'm having the toughest time.

I set my bag down on the ground and reached out with my hand, and she handed it to me. It was a purple grip, tacky to the touch, and I wrapped it around carefully.

Did it come with tape?

Her fingernails were dark red. She removed the thin overgrip tape from the paper and held it out for me. Thank you, she said, as I finished it off. Her eyes were a light brown and her voice was like syrup.

I've seen you, she said. You're a real player. Are you a pro? She crossed her legs as I stood over her.

Hardly, I said.

Did you recently join?

Not too long ago.

I want to watch you play more.

I may need to charge you, I said.

You could give me a lesson.

Maybe.

Her name was Carlin, and her hand felt warm in mine.

The way you played yesterday, you could have been a legend, the voice said. The voice, it was sounding more familiar, but I couldn't quite place it yet.

I heard you are captaining a team. How's the recruiting going?

It's going, I said.

Did you get Roland?

Not yet.

Good luck.

Why good luck?

Gun-shy, the voice said.

Aren't we all.

Keep hitting the gym. You still have a few pounds to shed. You should work out every day.

The heat was getting to me again.

Thanks for the advice, I said on my way out.

My wife was calling, but I pressed decline.

Was that Mom?

No, I said.

When we got to the club, I put my son in the childcare even though my ladder match wasn't for another 40 minutes—a guy named Forrest. He was #2 on the ladder, and I was #3.

The first thing I did was visualization. I found a loveseat upstairs by the bar in the corner of the room—no one there yet—and shut my eyes. I visualized each point of the match, my strategy in place.

I went to my locker and poured some talcum powder down my shorts. In the gym on the mat, I used the foam roller. Then I did some band work for my shoulders, my rotator cuff.

I drank some electrolytes. I ate a banana. I had my phone on airplane mode but still had Wi-Fi. I had three unread text messages from my wife. I pulled up YouTube and watched some behind-the-court footage of Marat Safin v. Roger Federer with my AirPods in my ears. I went back upstairs and did some yoga nidra. Then I took a shit.

Forrest was already on center court when I emerged from the locker room.

You're Forrest, I said. I'm Ned.

He gave me a nod, barely acknowledging me.

Got a can?

He showed me a can of Dunlop's. I didn't like those balls.

Mind if we use Penn?

Pro or Regular?

Regular.

Those balls fly a little.

Let's use your Dunlop's then, I said. It won't make a difference.

I had my tennis bag. I had a duffel with some salted peanuts, an extra towel, a hat, some wristbands, and more electrolyte mix should I need it. I had a big jug and a little jug. I set everything up on the high steps of center court, on the other side of the net from Forrest. I grabbed a freshly strung racquet out of my bag, unsheathed it, already regripped and dampened with a dampener, and I jogged around the court—high steps, butt kicks, side steps.

Up or down, I said, showing the butt of my handle as I eyed the building crowd. People were up by the bar on the balcony. There were some members gathering courtside by the tables. Seats were being pulled up. Drinks ordered. I saw Carlin and nearby was Thiago. He gave me a thumbs-up.

Don't we spin after the warm-up?

Let's just take care of it now.

Up, Forrest said.

I spun my racquet. It was up.

Serve or receive?

Receive.

Inspired choice, I said.

I pointed at the side I wanted and ran over. I saw Ken in the doorway of the main building, and I winked at him before I turned to face Forrest on the other side. He fed me a ball, and I ripped it back to him. He wasn't anticipating the speed. This was only the warm-up, but I needed to send him a message. The next ball came back to me even harder, and it was as if we were already mid-match, battling. I loved it.

The warm-up was fast paced, contentious, Forrest glaring at me in between rallies.

You think you can slow it down? he said.

I'm returning what you're giving, I said.

The match went according to plan. I was up 4–0.

At 30–15 on my serve, I kicked it out wide to his backhand. He was way off the court but managed to bunt it back. I wound up for a big forehand, but at the last second I changed the trajectory of my stroke and hit a dropper. Forrest sprinted hard, dashing for it, almost barreling into the net, and the head of his racquet scuffed the court as he tried to get under the ball before the second bounce—but he didn't. He froze.

He bent down and grabbed his left shin, his calf with both hands. He stood up straight and tried to walk. He was done.

You okay? I said as he limped around. He shook his head, looking down at the leg in question.

How serious is it?

I think I pulled something.

Fuck, I said. I meant it.

I was planning on asking Forrest to join the squad, but this injury would be at least a month-long setback I determined.

We shook hands at the net.

I looked around the court. All eyes were on me. I won. I won, and I was #2 on the ladder now. The second-best player at the club.

On my way out, I poked my head into Ken's office. He was seated behind his desk, reading glasses on, staring down at a ledger. He plucked his glasses off his face and sat back when he noticed me.

Impressive work out there, Ned, he said.

Thank you. I got a lucky break. Tough player, I said. It could have gone either way, I said.

He grabbed a blue-colored stapled packet and put his glasses back on.

Let's see. That puts you at—

#2.

That's right.

Who's Brent Barran.

He's the best player at this club, Ken said. College player. Young buck.

Sounds like a real stud.

He's out of town on a summer college circuit unfortunately. But maybe you can catch him when he's back.

I see, I said.

You're building quite a reputation for yourself as a real player, Ken said. I hope you go celebrate tonight. Take a day off tomorrow. You earned it.

No rest days for me, I said. But thank you.

When we got home, I pan-fried a rib eye. I seasoned it, ate it rare. I gave Freddie some ice cream. Then, I made myself an ice bath.

I removed my clothes and took a swig of Jose Cuervo before lowering myself into the icy water. It felt like a thousand tiny needles stabbing me at once. My heart rate was jacked. I grabbed the bottle and drank some more.

I gritted my teeth.

#2 soon to be #1.

Dear Loraine,

I read a recent study about how today's 20-year-olds have the same level of testosterone as men in their 70s. This is all to say that this young buck Brent Barran has low T. I won't shave for a few days, do a little bench press, and the kid will shit himself when I show up, guaranteed. He'll probably even have Mommy or Daddy chaperone him to the match.

Your husband is a stud, Loraine. Don't you ever forget that.

The next morning, I drove to the FedEx warehouse on Franklin. The warehouse itself was fenced off by a security gate that required a code. The elephant doors were open though, and I could see a conveyer belt that was temporarily halted and delivery trucks backed up alongside it. I spotted someone in a black-and-purple uniform trotting away on the other side.

Is Roland here? I called.

The person looked over their shoulder, kept walking.

Inside the shipping center, one person was in front of me. The man complained about a package that never arrived, that the so-called attempted delivery was a lie. He was home, by the door, the whole time, he said.

It's on a truck, he was told.

The man left in disgust, and I moved to the front of the line, where I met a Calvin.

Can I speak to the manager? I said, but Calvin was the manager.

The white lighting from above bounced off his bare head. His mouth was still arched in greeting with two deep dimples formed. Calvin was good at customer service.

When I asked for Roland, the dimples disappeared.

Roland no longer works here, he said.

Is this a recent change?

The man measured his words. Yes, he said.

What happened?

I am not at liberty to talk about it, he said.

He said, All I can say is Roland no longer works here.

Where are you? the voice said. It was my wife on Bluetooth. I looked at my son in the rearview, his mouth open, about to say something. I turned to him and raised my index finger to my lips. I mouthed *shh.*

Hello? she repeated.

We're running some errands.

Why would you do that?

What do you mean?

Bryce is at our house waiting. Playdate, remember? Katrina his mom just called me.

Well, where are you? I said.

I'm at work. Working.

We'll be there soon. Tell them to wait. I ended the call. I called Thiago. It rang three times.

Shit.

What, Dad?

I ended that call too.

Wait here, I said to my son.

No! I'm scared!

I got out of the car, slammed the door. His cries were muted, but I could still hear him. I passed by a member, someone I didn't know, an older woman in a visor. I nodded, and she didn't nod back, just looked at me.

Can you just buzz me in? I forgot my card, I said to the front desk.

Last name?

You know it already, I told the woman, rattled the locked waist-high gate. She pressed a button, and I pushed it open.

Out by center, I saw Thiago's bag resting atop a table. I looked around. He was by the ice machine scooping ice into a canteen.

Hey buddy, where's your stuff?

Give me 20? I forgot my racquets, I said. I live right around the corner.

Back at the car, my son had stopped crying but his cheeks were red, and I could see the trail of dried tears running down his face.

It's okay, I said as I put the car in reverse. Your friend is at the house.

When I pulled into the driveway, the mother Katrina was facing my incoming car with her arms crossed, her son with the mushroom cut seated at the steps. She was in a shawl cardigan the color of clay, and he had a white toy Ghostbusters car in his lap.

Sorry about that, I hollered from my open door.

We had a little bit of an emergency, I said, closing the door, approaching rapidly.

I walked to the lock, put in the key.

Sorry, sorry, sorry, I said, as I opened the door.

Bryce! Freddie is so happy to see you—right, Freddie? My son, he was perking up a little. He was right next to his friend. He was now holding the white Ghostbusters car.

What time should I pick him up? the mother said. She had a freckly face with hair parted down the middle, a normally friendly face.

Let's see, I said, checking my phone.

I had two texts from my wife and a text from Thiago.

How about three hours from now?

So, six o'clock.

Sure. Bryce can have dinner here if he likes. Right, Bryce?

Bryce looked up at me with his bright blue eyes.

I led the boys inside.

I told Katrina to text me if she had any concerns, but she stood by the door.

Okay, we got it under control. See you in a bit. I closed the door but didn't lock it. From the French blinds of the dining room, I watched her step away.

A few minutes went by. The boys were down on the ground on the rug playing with Hot Wheels. They were getting along just fine.

Hey! I announced. I'll tell you what.

Bryce looked at me, but my son didn't.

You guys want some pizza?! Bryce?!

Bryce was still looking at me, my son was not.

Sure, Dad, my son said as he pushed a black-and-purple hot rod onto an orange track.

Okay, I'll order some pizza right now!

I stepped into the kitchen and texted Thiago: *Be there in 5*

I came back into the living room.

So boys, listen up. I just spoke to the pizza place, Antonio's. Their delivery guys are all out. So that means I need to go get the pizza, okay?

I needed this hit with Thiago in order to keep my hot streak going. I had a reputation now. I needed to stay sharp.

I grabbed two apple juice boxes from the fridge. I grabbed two bags of Pirate's Booty. I set it up for the boys on the plastic blue kid's table.

I'll be right back, okay? I said. Freddie?

Yes, Dad, my son said.

Where am I going, Freddie? I said from the now open door.

To get pizza.

Right answer, son.

When I got to the club, Thiago was waiting for me on Court #6. I told him I only had time for a power hour. Drills and baseline games. I checked my phone every five minutes even though my son didn't have a way of reaching me.

You're hitting the ball well, Thiago said after the hit. Burgers and beers? he asked.

I gotta rush home, I said. My boy.

Here, I'll walk you out, and he walked beside me on the path bisecting the courts of the club. People were playing around us, but he wasn't looking and neither was I.

You're a good dad, he said as he watched the ground in front of him.

I don't know about that.

I see it, he said.

I could be employed.

Don't sell yourself short. You're giving him love. That's more important than money. Trust me, I know from experience.

Hey, thanks, man, I said. We were at the entrance of the club. My eyes were a little wet, and Thiago looked at me directly.

Battle again in a few days? he said. He stuck his fist out for a bump.

You got it, I said, bumping him back.

I pulled into the driveway.

You're a great father, I said to myself.

I climbed the front steps to the front door.

I put my key in the lock, then turned the key clockwise.

The front door yawned open and I stepped inside.

The living room was dark save the light of the TV. Both boys were reclined on the couch.

Dad, where were you? my son said keeping his eyes on the television.

Where's the pizza? my son said.

Dad?

Dad?

His name was Stefan. He looked like an eleven-year-old Agassi—the long, dirty-blond mullet like a lion's mane, the zippered polos with splashes of color, the short shorts over bright tights just above the knees. The father was rotund, with beady eyes. He had a job but was never at the job. He was always at his son's side. They both walked a little pigeon-toed. Stefan was the most prized student at the academy.

The academy was run by the brothers Bortnik. They were Russian. The older brother was Lazar and the younger brother was Bogden.

My old man took me to the trial lesson. Bogden fed the balls and Lazar watched me from behind. I could hear his heavy breathing—he was a large man.

Good, he said to me occasionally.

When the basket was empty, Lazar lumbered slowly over to his brother on the other side of the court like a bear coming out of sleep. They conferred, Bogden's eyes on me, Lazar speaking into his brother's ear. Then, unceremoniously, slowly, Lazar left the court.

We'll take him, Bogden said to my old man.

I picked up the balls.

The next day my mother dropped me off at the academy. When I arrived, players were already jogging around the courts. The academy had three courts side by side with no barriers between. No one was walking, talking, or smiling. Roland was one of the players. He nodded at me as he ran by.

Let's go, let's go, Bogden said to me, snapping his fingers. I put my bag down, my water jug, and I started running.

After we did a circle stretch led by Bogden in the center—toe touches, quad stretches, back arches—people were named in pairs.

Roland and Christopher, Court 5, Bogden said.

Finally, it was just Stefan and me.

Stefan, take Ned to the hot seat, Bogden said. His eyes sparkled a little, and his mouth looked slightly devilish.

Lazar was nowhere in sight.

Stefan chuckled.

What happens when he loses?

The loser always suffers the same fate, Bogden said.

I heard a man's laughter off-court and turned to see Stefan's father behind the gate.

Lead the way, Stefan, Bogden said, and with that Stefan shouldered his bag, his big blue thermos, and marched off like he was about to enter center court at Wimbledon.

I followed Stefan up metal stairs that rumbled and shook with each step. We took a narrow path with fences on either side wrapped in Bougainvillea. He still hadn't said a word to me.

When we got to the court, I noticed the cameras right away. There were two camcorders each mounted on the highline of both fences on opposite sides of the court, right behind the baseline. I saw a tiny green light like a little eye on each.

I noticed his father behind me. He passed by like a shark scoping its prey and took a seat on the bench, the one I was going to sit on. I put my stuff down on the ground instead and laid a towel next to it—where I planned to sit.

We had a brusque warm-up. When I came to net to hit some volleys, it felt like he was hitting the ball as hard as he could right at me. The balls came like bullets. I only took one overhead, and then we jumped into serves.

By the time the match started, I had lost my nerve. I couldn't keep the ball in. It was like I forgot how to play the game, like I was hypnotized.

We only played a set, but it was over in twenty minutes.

I only won three points.

When the set was over, waiting there at the gate was Bogden. Stefan left with his father without shaking my hand, and Bogden entered. He lifted a tall hook ladder resting on its side. He raised the ladder and leaned it against the fence closest to him, the hooks hooking over the top. He climbed until he was at the camcorder, removing the evidence of my demise.

Follow me, Bogden said moments later with the cassette in hand.

Bogden led me to a parking lot where a trailer stood. The trailer was dark inside, musty, the windows gauzed in cloth blinds. It reeked of vodka, and there was a hulking figure resting in a bed in the back. Before the bed was a round table with a circular bench wrapped around it.

Sit here, Bogden said, and I sat down on the dark-red cushion.

There was a TV monitor up high, and I looked at the black screen. Then, it turned on. Lazar was behind me and on the screen was the match I just played, the warm-up. Bogden left us there, and I didn't dare look behind me. I could hear his breathing. My neck felt tight. I could feel the cold sweat dripping down my sides from my armpits. It was twenty minutes but felt much longer. Every time Lazar coughed, I jumped. It was phlegmy, loud. When he sneezed, I peed myself a little.

The recording ended. The image went static. I didn't move. I didn't know what to do. I knew Lazar was there, but he didn't move either.

You play like a real pussy. You know that?

Yes, I said.

Then, I heard the mattress creak.

Come with me.

When we arrived at the courts, everyone was there waiting. They were standing on the far court, racquets held to their chests, all eyes on me. The middle court was mine. Lazar walked over to a basket full of balls, a feeding racquet on top of the pile. Bogden saw my uncertainty and pointed to the other side, the baseline opposite Lazar.

Over there, he said.

When I got to the center mark I had barely turned around before a ball was coming at me. I hit a forehand on the run. Then, Lazar fed another ball to the opposite alley. I ran it down for a backhand.

You will do this 200 times, Bogden said. Back and forth. These are called suicides.

We stop when you reach 200 or when you puke. Whatever comes first.

And if you hit like a pussy, you start over, Lazar boomed.

Lazar started counting from one. I ran my ass off.

Out of the corner of my eye, the other players of the academy stood statuesque. By the time I had reached nineteen, I was gagging, but nothing was coming out yet.

Eighteen, Lazar said as he fed another untouched ball.

He kept feeding as I was keeled over. Snot was coming out of my nose, and my left calf was cramping.

Fifteen, he said. He was going backwards because I had stopped.

I began to cry.

When he reached ten, I started running again, but two dead sprints found me at the back fence. This time the remnants of my lunch—a peanut butter sandwich with grape jelly—slapped the court.

A towel was dropped next to me, a spray bottle with disinfectant.

Welcome to the academy, Bogden said.

When I got home that evening, my old man told me I should be grateful.

The next day I showed up at the academy. We started off by hitting serves. Bogden stood behind us, tossing the balls for us to use, one serve at a time. When we missed, Bogden pitched fast balls into the center of our backs.

In the mirror that night, I studied my welts.

I wish I had this opportunity when I was your age, my old man said to me before bed.

A week later, done with stretches again, our names were called, players disappearing in pairs to their assigned courts.

Finally, it was just Roland and me standing.

Hot-seat time, Bogden said, winking at me.

I gathered my bag, my jug of water. My hands—they were shaking.

Hurry, Bogden said.

When we reached the court, before we entered, I felt Roland's hand fall on my shoulder. We were under a canopy, shadowed, but I could still see his clear blue eyes. He looked calm, confident.

Don't worry, he said.

The green eyes of the camcorders were trained down on us.

We warmed up slowly, methodically. I wasn't sure what was happening, but I felt at ease again.

Start the match, a voice came from behind the windscreen. Then the dark silhouette disappeared.

Roland spun his racquet, and I called up. It was up. I elected to receive. I faced the service box. Roland bounced the ball, once, twice, then tossed the ball and swung so hard that it hit the back fence, not far from where Bogden had previously stood.

Second serve, and the ball slammed against the back fence again.

I studied Roland's face, but he didn't crack.

Are you okay? I said.

Love-fifteen, he said, bouncing the ball on the ad side, ready to serve. I lifted my racquet head up and settled into the ready position. I split-stepped as he struck the ball, the fence behind me pinging again as he hit it straight-on.

Roland double-faulted the whole game at love.

During the changeover, I asked if everything was okay.

Yup, Roland said. He was all business.

And then when it came to my serve, every return of his hit the back fence or the bottom of the net.

The match was over in fifteen minutes. Roland gave me the match—a gift.

I watched Roland walk off the court to the trailer, Bogden shutting the trailer door behind them.

When Roland appeared on the courts below, his right cheek was bright red, but his eyes were dry. We were all lined up on the far court waiting, my position reversed from Roland's a week ago. He approached the baseline in his blue-and-white Adidas, the center mark. It began. He was already dashing side to side, Bogden behind him, Lazar feeding bullets alley to alley. I was next to Stefan.

You're very lucky, Stefan said. Next time you won't be.

Roland tracked every ball down, his feet screeching and sliding as his racquet connected, then pivoting and flying to the other side, to the next feed.

When he reached 112, he stopped suddenly and vomited. It was a silent vomit, but it poured out of him. But then Roland stood up straight. Ready position.

By the time he reached 200, he had puked two more times. It ended unceremoniously. No claps, no cheers, nothing. Roland swayed there at the baseline like a fighter, a boxer after twelve rounds.

After Lazar left, I bent down and slid a protein bar to Roland.

I wanted to say something, to thank him, but I didn't need to. He knew.

Back at the club, after I swiped my keychain card that I kept not on my keychain but hidden inside my wallet, I rounded the corner and almost ran into Roland.

This was the first time I saw his face—the last two times it had been covered. His chin was clefted and the point of his nose was slightly bulbous. His eyebrows were in a thoughtful arch, and his mouth slightly parted as if he just said something or was about to say something. His hair was straw blond and long enough to reveal its natural curly nature, but short enough to create an upright crown. His eyes though—they were blue like I remember, but there was something drained about them, like they had seen enough of this life.

Roland, hey man. Its Ned, I said, in case he forgot. He nodded at me, didn't say a word, and didn't appear alarmed by my presence. He simply stopped. His shoulders were wide. I filled in the silence. I didn't know how much time I had.

I'm forming a men's league team out of the club. Matches start in a week and a half, and the season runs through the summer. The format is one singles and two doubles lines. Are you busy Sundays?

He shook his head. No, he said. He looked away.

I want you on my team.

I waited until his eyes met mine.

Can I count you in?

Okay, he said, but doubles only.

Got it. Doubles only.

Then, like that, Roland was on the squad. He walked past and headed for the exit, and I went to the daycare to retrieve my son.

Roland was the #1 player in the country in every division—boys 10s, 12s, 14s, 16s. He started playing up, competing against boys two–three years older. It didn't matter. Roland always found a way.

In high school, I fell in love with his sister. She drove a black BMW convertible, and we had French class together. I'd sit behind her, and she'd let me see her answers. She'd flip her hair back, and I'd smell the shampoo she used.

I'd watch him in the gym, doing bicep curls in a surf-brand tank top with a sixty-pound bar. His arms were tan. He'd be in there with his friends, other surfers and skaters from high school. He got in with the wrong crowd, but he still kept it together. I saw him skate by once—he hadn't seen me—at the pier. He kicked the tail of his board into his hand and leaned over the rails. He was parallel to the surf and whistled at someone, a girl he knew, a surfer. She melted when she saw him watching her. She caught the wave of the day after that. He was the golden boy. Nothing could touch him.

Nothing could touch Roland—except one thing.

I submitted my final roster to the official organization by the Friday deadline with our first match scheduled to occur the following Sunday:

Thiago
Bray
The Podiatrist Snider
Roland
Myself
Stout

Burris. He was the shirt ripper. He seemed amiable enough, strolling on the court with an upbeat K-Swiss–shoed gait. One peculiarity was he kneeled down next to the net, face alongside it as if he was speaking into its ear, with one hand gently stroking its tautness like the strings of a guitar. His lips moved, whispering—I could not hear a single word, and I didn't know him well enough to ask him what he was saying. Our warm-up was standard and collaborative, hitting to each other down the center. Then, we played a series of super tiebreakers, and after I won the last one at love, he proceeded to tear his collarless polo right down the center until it was no longer a shirt but a vest. His chest was bare and hairless like a boy's, and when he shook my hand at the net, his smile and his happy nature resumed. He walked out of the club wearing the remnants of his clothing, and I received a text from him later that night confirming his availability for the summer league.

We played in the rain for our first team practice. I purchased a case of balls and a hopper the day prior. Burris, Thiago, Snider, Stout, Bray—everyone was in attendance except Roland. When the balls became too soaked, I went over to the closet room with the washer and dryer the facility used to clean the towels.

I put the balls in the dryer on high for five minutes, something my old man used to do when we'd play when it was wet.

I hand-tossed balls to my men. They moved around me like water coming out of two fountain spouts, hitting and rotating in perfect unison as I tossed to either side of me.

Afterward we ran lines, touching each one. We stretched in a circle.

In the locker room, most of my men shaved and showered. I didn't bring a change of clothes. I pulled the elastic band of my shorts open and poured some talcum powder. Then I slipped into some slides and met everyone at a round table near the bar. Draft beer and buttered popcorn in red-and-white checkered paper trays covered the wood.

Here is the lineup for Sunday, I said, standing. I removed the folded paper from my pocket, a sheet from a yellow legal pad I had at home where I kept my team notes.

Now, everyone will get a chance to play this season. So, if you're sitting out this time around, don't be alarmed. I looked at Stout in his cashmere sweater polo, and his mouth seemed to downturn when our eyes met.

Thiago, you'll play singles. Bray, you'll be doubles line one with Roland.

I looked over at Snider, Burris.

Snider and Burris, you'll be our line-two doubles. I folded the paper.

Let's get fired up, team! Burris said, raising his glass.

The other players raised theirs except Stout—from the corner of my eye, I saw him make for the stairs leading to the exit.

Stout, I said, following, but he marched out in his steel-blue, suede driving shoes.

It was sometime in November. The days were getting shorter, and Roland was on center court playing against a D1 college player in the club tournament. Roland was the #1 eighteen-year-old in the country and set to play for coach Dick Gould at Stanford. The paperwork was provisional, but it had already been signed.

They were in a first-set tiebreaker and Roland came to net behind an up-the-line forehand approach. His opponent barely got to the ball—all he could do was send it up in the air for an easy put-away. Roland—he somehow framed the overhead. The ball flew out of the court into a nearby patch of grass. He lost the tiebreaker and the set, and as he approached his water bottle, he began to smash his racquet into pieces. His face was calm, stoic, but full of blood. He kept going until all he held was the handle itself. There were racquet shards all over the court, sparkling like broken glass. He lost the next set 6–0 in twenty minutes.

I found out after the match that his mother had been diagnosed with stage-4 breast cancer, and it had spread to her brain.

She would die soon.

I had just put my son to bed when Burris the shirt-ripper called. I was downstairs in the kitchen.

Are you sure Bray at #1 doubles is the right call?

You and Snider play well together. You have a history together. I checked your league records.

So put us at #1, Burris said.

Roland is our doubles ringer though.

Put me with Roland then instead of Bray. I beat Bray last week.

Singles is a different game than doubles.

There was a pause. With the phone sandwiched between my cheek and shoulder, I filled a kettle with water. In a mug nearby was an unwetted bag of Ashwagandha tea to relax the mind. I needed to be calm, steady, as captain.

We're going with the lineup—

I took a video of the match against Bray. Check your messages. I texted you the link.

I set the kettle on the stove and turned the burner to high. The flames licked the sides and singed a drop of water that slid down the black kettle.

Watch the video, he said.

The lineup stands as is.

I respectfully disagree with that decision. Are you going to watch the video?

Good night, Burris.

At the #2 line, there's a greater chance for my rating to go down.

It's a team effort, Burris. Good night, I repeated.

I hung up the phone.

When the tea was ready, I settled on the couch and clicked the link. It took me to a YouTube channel called *Burris the Tennis Baller*. There were at least fifty videos, all tennis, all of Burris playing other members of the club. I scrolled up and down. I found the one titled

"Burris against Bray 6/14." There was some overlaid commentary from Burris:

"This is the fifth time this year Bray and I have sparred at the Wind & Sea Tennis Facility. And spoiler alert—this is the fifth match I won. Undefeated, babyyyyyyy."

I skipped ahead. Burris lobbed Bray over his head at net to win one point. Burris forced a backhand error with a heavy deep ball to win another point. Defensive tennis. I wasn't impressed. I skipped to the end. Bray approached the camera and gave it the middle finger. Then, from the bird's-eye view, Bray bisected the court to the side gate. He left without shaking Burris' hand.

Then, the video went black.

Dear Loraine,

Men are hard to please.

I was already dressed and ready to go. I had a little product in my hair, a little stubble—the way my wife liked it.

Ruby the sitter arrived, and I walked her to the kitchen, showed her the plated sandwich in the fridge, pointed at the milk, the yogurt, and emphasized his bedtime: 8 P.M. I didn't show her the toothbrush. I didn't show her the Q-tips, the bubble bath products, the sponge.

But when my wife came down the stairs in a nice summer dress, she showed Ruby the toothbrush and toothpaste, the Q-tips, the bubble bath products, the sponge. She pointed to the baby carrots in the fridge, the broccoli, the apple sauce. She said 8:30 for the bedtime.

The restaurant was one of those hole-in-the-wall deals on the outside, a shitty strip mall on a busy street—not enough parking, next to a pet store, a donut shop, a liquor store, a taco stand. The restaurant was Michelin rated.

We were seated across from each other at a polished dark-wood table. It was perfect, us together again, alone. Like old times.

We regarded the menus placed below us.

Wow, she said, and I smiled expectantly. But then she said it, the E word, killing the whole vibe.

Expensive, she said.

It's date night, honey, I said. Don't worry about it.

There. My attempt to restore the balance. I reached across the table and covered her hand in mine. She left it there, but then she pulled away, and held the menu with both hands.

No, it looks amazing, honey. It's just a little pricey is all. That's okay, she said, smiling at me.

It felt like a corporate smile. The smile HR gives you after you complete a mandatory training.

That's okay, I repeated.

She took a second to digest that, then her nose smarted a little.

Are you mocking me?

No, why would you say that?

And the waiter arrived just in time. He listed off the specials—a pan-seared striped bass, a blue-crab spaghetti. He didn't say the price and my wife didn't ask. He looked at her as if she held the wallet of the family. He was right.

Can I start you off with something to drink?

Just a water.

Sparkling or—

Flat, my wife said. Flat is fine.

I'll have the house Cab, I said. I looked at the waiter. Then, I looked down at the table. I could see my reflection on the cut glass covering the wood.

When I looked at my wife again, a server came over with two glasses of water. They were placed before us. My wife, she looked composed again. A new page.

I think I'm getting the smoked chicken. What about you?

I was thinking either the steak Diane or one of the specials. My wife, she looked at me a little sideways.

Or the burger, I said.

I ended up ordering the burger.

No dessert.

The next morning, my wife was already gone by the time I woke up. She was at the airport.

I got up and made my son breakfast.

Within the cage of the power rack, I saw her. She was clad in cobalt high-rise tights and a matching sports bra. Perched behind her head was a weightlifting bar with a plate balanced on each side. She was in a deep squat, her eyes zeroed in ahead. Then standing straight with grace, she stepped forward and released the bar within the hooks of the rack. Her arms were perfectly tan, matching the shade of her visible bare waist, not a tan line in sight. She was breathing hard, and she turned her head and saw me. She recognized me. Her lips, they smiled at me. She wore pearl earrings, and her hair was in a taut high pony. She took care of herself.

Why are you staring at her? my son said.

I led him to the childcare center, opened the door.

At the long bar, on the second-to-last stool sat Roland with a pint of something dark. His shoulders were wide in his poncho hoodie. A basketball game aired on the mounted flatscreen, the changing light reflecting on the polished counter. Two members sat farther down. Roland didn't watch the TV, didn't talk to the others. He sat there alone. I didn't even see him touch his drink.

Roland pretty much quit tennis after his mother's diagnosis. He dedicated himself full-time to skating and surfing. He skipped class. I didn't see him for months.

His sister also stopped showing up to school. She fell in with the party crowd.

Their mother died at home after four months, never making it to hospice. That afternoon, Roland showed up in his Econoline with the basket of balls. He was calm, polite, said hello when he passed me, and took one of the backcourts. He hit basket upon basket of serves—we could hear the succession of balls pounding the green heavy-duty windscreen. The club turned the lights on for him when night came, and he kept serving. He kept serving until closing time.

The morning before the first league match, I received an email from the organization. The message did not start off with a greeting:

In response to a filed grievance against Thiago Jerome, the ratings committee has judged that Mr. Jerome is too advanced for the current league. Mr. Jerome has been removed from your roster for this season. In the Winter, there is a higher category that Mr. Jerome is eligible for.

Thiago was supposed to play singles for us. I called him and shared the bad news. I texted Stout to see if he was still available. *Too late*, he wrote. *You should have thought of that before sitting me out.*

I'd have to put myself in. I'd have to play.

And Roland, if we wanted to win, he'd have to play singles.

That night, leaving the club, my son's hand in mine, we walked to my car at the far end of the parking lot. The lot was dark. Leaning against the passenger side of a van with a back bumper held together by bungee cords was a man, his back to us. His shoulders were shivering, and I saw an unsteady hand rise with the red glow of a cigarette. The man brought it to his mouth, but he still shivered. He choked on some smoke, and that's when I heard the sob. He keeled over slightly with the sob, and as we neared, it was clear that the man was crying. The cigarette fell and his face fell too, right into his hands. The man, he shouted through his hands.

What's wrong with him? my son said, and I shushed him.

Get in the car, I said softly, and I strapped my son to his booster, closed his door gently.

On the car ride home, my son didn't ask me any more questions. I kept the radio off, drove straight.

The man was Roland.

One day, after a lesson, my coach pulled me aside. He told me that Roland was no longer a member of the club. I asked why, and he didn't give me any good reason.

What happened was this.

The family had a dog, a Belgian Malinois. The dog had been in the sister's room, barking uncontrollably. Roland was the only one home. When Roland entered the room, he found the dog nudging and barking at a drawer from his sister's chest. Roland yanked the drawer open. Beneath some socks he found the cocaine.

Roland knew the dealer. It was a small town. He threw his skateboard in the back of his Econoline and drove to the boardwalk. He parked the car as close as he could without putting money in the meter and skated hard. He kept skating and skating and skating, past the bars, restaurants, trinket shops, taco stand, bait & tackle, the Hawaiian ice shop until he saw who he was looking for. And he didn't slow down. He skated right into him. He promised his dying mother that he would watch over his little sister. Roland pinned him down on the ground, raised his skateboard over his head deck down, and slammed it over and over again. Then, he dragged the still-breathing body to the curb—the head. Cantaloupe.

Roland served a sentence, got out, and then served another sentence for something else. I never saw him again.

I kept playing until my freshman year of college. I made it to a midlevel D1 program as a walk-on. I played 5 or 6 in the lineup until the incident.

I had no reason to play after that.

I quit tennis for fourteen years.

The next morning, I woke up at 5 A.M. I made myself a French press coffee, and the burr grinder woke my son. I toasted some waffles for him. I broke the waffle into pieces by hand. Then I poured maple syrup, and he complained that I poured too much. By 7 A.M., I switched to the Chemex and made a second batch of the Sumatran using a brown filter, unbleached. I toasted the heel piece of cracked sourdough and ate it without butter. I had to go to the bathroom frequently. I did some pushups on the hardwood to ground myself. There was a dense fog outside—the air was misting. I called the club. The courts were wet. I put on some sunscreen. I watched the highlights from Halle, a warm-up grass-court tournament before Wimbledon. I ate a protein bar. I made myself a smoothie with dried mango, arugula, peanut butter, ice, and 2%. I poured it into the sink after one sip. I messaged my squad: *Match still on for noon, courts should be dry.* I tied the end of a red band around the sliding door handle like a tourniquet and proceeded to tug it in various ways as part of my rotator cuff exercise regimen. When we arrived at the club, it was 10 A.M. The courts were soaked, no one playing, and the toy room was locked. When I gave it a knock, no one answered.

Childcare is closed on Sundays, the front desk told me.

10:07. From the stretching mat, I texted every babysitter in my contacts, my son next to me with his iPad. Helena could be there by 11.

When we arrived back home, the dining room chandelier glowed through the faux-wood blinds. I didn't remember opening the blinds. I didn't remember keeping the lights on.

As I unlocked the door, her voice descended to our ears—my wife was home, on the second floor, her footfalls landing on the stairs.

Surprise!

Mommy! Frederick said, running into her arms. She was draped in a brown oversized cashmere cardigan. Her hair was in a lazy pony.

You're back from your trip, I said.

Where were you guys?

At the park. I looked at my son and his eyes met mine in what I interpreted as understanding. He didn't say anything.

I have a babysitter coming at 11, I said, remembering.

Oh? Why?

I'm meeting with some friends.

Her eyes fell away as she knelt down to tidy up—action figures, Hot Wheel cars, puzzle pieces covering the washable reversible rug in our living room area. She didn't seem suspicious.

I'm playing tennis with Gio and Carter.

You're playing tennis again? My wife sounded alarmed. I could sense it.

Just for fun, I said.

I said, Do you want me to cancel the babysitter?

Sure. Right, Freddie? My wife looked at my son.

My son said, Yeah.

My son said, I want some mommy time.

Great, I said. Well if you don't mind, I'm going to head out now to pick up some balls. Frederick, come help get your backpack, I said.

You get it, he said.

Go help your daddy, Freddie, and my son listened.

In the driveway again, I opened the passenger side. My wife—I could see her through the dining room windows—was in the living room just beyond, still cleaning up.

Now, remember our agreement.

Don't tell Mom about the club.

That's right.

Well, you better get me another toy then. My son's eyes were a cold bright blue. He didn't blink as he waited for my response.

What do you want? I said.

10:56. When I pulled into the club parking lot, sunlight appeared. The clouds were breaking apart, the marine layer starting to burn. The front desk handed me a warm towel. I pressed it against my cheek.

I found Roland in the locker room. He was bent over his shoes, seated on a bench, lacing up. His eyelids looked full, heavy.

Courts are still wet, I said.

I asked, Want to warm up our volleys on one of the racquetball courts?

He carried two racquets in his hand by their throats. He wore a black nylon drawstring backpack. He didn't have a water. We entered the racquetball facility and found an empty chamber behind the indoor basketball court. I threw him a couple used Penns and he leaned one racquet against the wall and bounced one of the balls with the other.

Listen, I said, as I stood opposite him. Thiago can't play today. He hit a ball gently to me, and I volleyed it back in kind.

What that means, I said, is I need to put you in singles. The next ball grazed the frame of his racquet, sending it behind him.

I know you only wanted to play doubles. But we don't have any other options. And you're our best chance to win at singles. He turned away slowly to get the ball. Everything he did was slow, like he was barely functioning.

I haven't played a competitive match since high school, he said.

We're in the same boat, I told him. He hit the ball to me, and we volleyed again until I missed it. He walked over to his other racquet and leaned back against the wall. He sunk down to the ground until he was seated, and with the racquet between his legs, he straightened his strings.

How are you feeling? I said.

Fine, he said. He was concentrating on his strings. I hit some backhand volleys against the wall. Then, he put the racquet down next to him and reached for the other, repeating his string straightening, plucking them until he was satisfied. He grabbed a pack of Cabo Golds from his baggy basketball shorts. He flicked his lighter, smoked one, and then another, ashing them out on the ground.

The air became clouded. The smoke was stuck—nowhere to go.

I'm a little nervous, I said. I waited for him to say something, but he didn't. He looked down at his hands—they were strong hands downed in tufts of hair.

I saw you last night, in the parking lot, I said. He kept looking at his hands.

I said, Everything okay?

He nodded.

I'm here if you want to talk, okay?

He nodded again.

Do you want me to get you a water?

He shook his head.

I'm okay, he said.

At the snack shop, I got him one anyways, and a red Gatorade too, but the racquetball court was empty when I returned. Just my bag and a few scattered balls. I snatched one and smacked it against the high ceiling.

I picked up his cigarette butts and threw them away.

The other captain was a man in a red visor named Maddock. He showed up with his five guys at 11:50—ten minutes prior to the match. Maddock wore one of those backpack chairs normally used at the beach. He carried a cooler with him. He was a head shorter than me, but stocky, and he walked quickly. His nose was coated with zinc oxide and I could see a few strands of white here and there in his otherwise bushy red beard. His whole team was dressed in black athletic tees and shorts, and they all appeared only a few years out of college. In other words, they looked fit and ready to play. Our three assigned courts were in full view from the balcony that spilled out from the bar, and there was also a set of bleachers on two of the courts.

Bummer about your guy Thiago, Maddock said to me as we exchanged the lineup. I was on the court now, and he was on the other side of the short fence. The fence stopped at my chest, his chin.

A real ringer. Definitely too good for this league.

Had you seen him play before? I asked as I straightened my strings.

I looked up his stats. I ran the numbers. I was the one who filed a grievance against him.

I see, I said.

I shifted over to the ad side of the court, my partner Phil Bray in the deuce. Maddock turned his back to me.

Let's go, boys! he called to his men on the other court.

To my left on the adjacent court was Roland. His face, like the last time I saw him play, was fully covered. All I could see were his eyes.

By 3-all in the first set of our doubles match, the balcony above was covered in faces, sun umbrellas, and tables with shiny golden beer and pitchers overflowing with margaritas. Burris and Snider were in a battle, and Roland, judging by his opponents' occasional shouts, was in the lead. All was going according to plan.

Then what happened was this: Roland, during my changeover, had an easy put-away volley that he dumped in the net followed by a missed approach shot, and then a double fault. Errors always happen, that is part of the game. But then a fan from up above, a wheelchaired man with long silver hair, raised both of his hands in the air in exasperation and yelled down.

Come on! You know how to play tennis, don't you?

Roland took notice, I could tell. He looked up at this heckler defiantly, but then something came across him, a shadow of something, and strangely a swift-moving cloud passed over the sun in that exact moment, making everything appear still and lifeless. I met Roland's eyes—they reminded me of my son's eyes.

Ignore him, I said.

The game continued, and it was my duty to play my match, to be present mentally and physically, but I couldn't help but keep my eyes and ears on Roland. I wasn't on my court—I was on Roland's. The crowd above seemed to distance themselves from the heckler to the point where no one else was hovering above Roland's match. Just this sole man in the wheelchair, slapping his leg and shouting at every missed shot.

Too much spin! he'd yell at one point.

Move your feet! he'd yell after another. You're flat-footed!

Toss the ball higher! when Roland was serving. Who was this tormenter, this plague?

Our court was about to start the tiebreaker when, over to my right, Burris came up with a put-away poach to solidify their first set—a small crowd cheered. I swiveled my head to Roland as he was mid-service motion, a second presumably because of the kick, and he followed behind it daringly but slowly to the net, where the return of serve passed by him, just out of reach, down-the-line. His opponent in a bandana with long white tails and a cut-off black tee gave an uppercut punch in celebration.

Thata way, Joshie, Maddock cheered in my other ear, out of my line of sight. Roland with his head down walked to the bench when the final assault came.

You call yourself a tennis player? You're just a hack now!

A hack! the voice came again.

I'm going to call a time violation on your court. I could hear Maddock utter these words to me, but I was walking away from him to Roland. Roland was standing still, knees a little bent as if to sit, regarding his tormenter, frozen. With one hand, he ripped off his mask, and his face was a deep red, his jaw clenched. He's going to hit a ball at him, I thought. He's going to throw his racquet at him. He's going to climb the steps and throw this man overboard.

Oh, how far you have fallen! How far you have fallen! the man said. Roland grabbed his two racquets, stuffed his face covering into his pocket, and left the court. I didn't chase after him. I had to play—for the team. I let him go.

We lost the first-set tiebreaker after that.

At the beginning of the second, I looked up at the balcony and saw her there—Carlin. She was in a forest-green zip-front collared dress, with her hand resting under her chin, her elbow supported by the railing. She looked at me thoughtfully, and I detected a mild smile. I suddenly felt light. My partner was serving, and the first point I decided to poach—I didn't even give a signal for it, I just pounced for a stab volley that went between the legs of the net guy on the other side. I didn't look up—I knew she was watching. I knew she was impressed.

We found a rhythm. We broke serve the next game, and I held the following. We took the set and found ourselves up in the deciding super tiebreaker with points to spare. Maddock from the bleachers, questioned one of my calls, and I responded in kind with an ace out wide. The opponents shook our hands, zipped up their bags, and left. Burris and Snider had already won in straight sets. Bray and I were the clinchers.

Carlin was no longer on the balcony.

When I went up to the bar, other members sloshed and shoulder-squeezed and back-slapped and bar-tabbed me. I split a pitcher of a Doppelbock with Bray, Snider, and Burris. I ate some fried pickles and a soft pretzel. I felt like a winner, a champion, a king, like I had been knighted after winning Wimbledon.

I found Ken in his office, parked at his desk. He was lost in thought, looking at the wall—a toile wallpapered stick-and-peel deal of a fox-hunt. His arm was sling-free now.

He didn't know who the man was, the one in the wheelchair, but I followed him to the front desk, where we checked the guest log. I described the man to the front desk girl as we scanned the sign-in sheet.

Oh, she said while consulting the computer. Him.

She said, He's a member. Last name Belter, first name Vernon.

Belter is Roland's last name, Ken said.

Vernon Belter was Roland's father.

I drank the last drop of water before starting the car. I was good enough to drive. It took me five minutes to get home, and the house itself, it looked different, maybe the gardener came finally when I was gone, maybe he trimmed the trees. I walked up to the lock and tried to put my key in the hole, but the key, it wouldn't insert. I tried another, and then another. Finally, I used the lionhead door knocker.

A woman, not my wife, answered. She didn't open the door all the way. In fact, it was latched.

Yes?

I took a step back. I noticed the gabled roof, the turrets, the towers, the stained glass.

I'm so sorry, I said.

I got back in the car and drove away from my childhood home.

Dear Loraine,

Upon your return from Provo, we attended as a family Alabaster's birthday party at the park. As you may recall, an ice-cream truck pulled up and even though the party had cake and cupcakes, you relented because Frederick was beginning to make a scene and allowed him to have the Choco Taco he desired. Fine. I chose harmony over discord any day of the week. That is not the issue at hand. The issue was the man, a father I do not know, with a beard that looked like beaver fur. The ice-cream truck was cash only, and neither of us had cash. I told you I could go to the ATM at the liquor store across the road, but instead, this man offered you, not me, the cash, and you accepted it. I thought this was a rather intrusive and inappropriate gesture on his part, yet you gladly accepted it. Your fingers might have even touched his in the exchange. This reminds me of the time when we were quarrelling at an outdoor concert, when we were trying to picnic together before the show began, when another man had some half-finished charcuterie he offered us, namely you, and you took it. You took the plastic tray from him without hesitation to spite me. What happens next? If our AC stops working, will you go live with our neighbor? If my down jacket, the one you always steal, has a hole in it, will you take the coat of another man? If I get a flat tire, will you hitch a ride with someone else and leave me there? If my dick stops working, will you gallop onto another?

Yours,
N.

I left a voicemail for Roland. I wanted to check in on him. We needed him for our next match.

You're doing it wrong, I said to my son. You're not listening.

I fed him another ball. He was at the service line, and I was trying to show him the fundamentals—low to high, swing all the way through, semi-western grip for the forehand.

Dad, can we stop?

No, I said. I fed him another ball.

Swing through the ball, I said. He hit it in the net.

Bend your knees, I said.

Nothing was working. I grabbed the basket and carried it to the other side of the net. My son was in Velcro shoes, tiny socks that were too short, basketball shorts that were too long, a Pokémon T-shirt. His hair was in his eyes, and he brushed it aside. His eyes, they looked a little wet. Forge ahead, I thought.

He needs to learn, I thought.

I shifted him by the shoulders back to the center line of the service line. He didn't like that.

Here, I said, grabbing from the basket and tossing him another ball.

Better, I said. But I jinxed it. He reverted back to his slap, right into the net, opening the shoulders too fast, not moving his feet.

What's wrong with you? I said.

Can't you listen?

I was yelling.

He was crying now, and the people on the court next to us, they were looking.

I picked up the balls quickly and he followed me out of the club to the car silently.

I turned on the car and put it in reverse once he was buckled. I turned on the radio, turned up the sound. I looked at him in the rearview. He was staring out the window, mouth shut. I saw my own reflection in the mirror.

Piece of shit, I thought to myself.

You piece of shit, I thought again as I made eye contact with myself. I looked away. It wasn't his fault. It was my fault. My ears felt hot all of the sudden, my shoulders heavy.

I'm sorry, I said over the music.

I looked at myself again.

I'm fucking sorry, I said.

I pounded the steering wheel with my fist. It honked.

Dad, why are you crying?

I'm not crying!

Why are there tears then?

I wiped my face. I blew my nose into a crunched-up napkin I found in one of the cupholders of the center console.

Allergies. I'm sorry!

Dad, it's okay! I forgive you.

I took a deep breath, turned on the left blinker at the light.

I forgive you, Dad, my son said.

When we got home, I poured myself some bourbon. I gave my son his iPad. I roasted some baby potatoes—all the adult food we had—and ate them with a half-finished bottle of Beaujolais that was sitting out. My son, he had a feast—he ate an Uncrustable, a bag of Cheetos, a pink lemonade popsicle. He asked for a cookie, and I gave him the last Snickerdoodle.

Want ice cream? I said.

Sure, he said, smiling from the couch. I got him an ice cream cone, the one with hard chocolate covered in nuts doming the vanilla. I gave him some milk. I gave him a hug.

You don't need to be a tennis player like me, I said.

Okay, Dad, he said.

If you change your mind, let me know, I said. You might change your mind.

But my son, he didn't change his mind.

I went over to Stout's private practice, his law office. It looked rural, like a home—a green roof, a screen door, French shutters on either side of the windows. There was even a table and two chairs outside like the outdoor seating of a café. When I stepped inside, I was met by his secretary, a woman in a teal flared-sleeve shirt. She asked if I could take a seat. I sat in an armchair and fingered a couple magazines.

He's ready to see you now.

She led me to his office, where he sat behind his executive desk in a dimpled leather chair. Behind him was a bookcase with thick legal volumes and encased autographed tennis balls. The dual picture frame that stood like an upright open book featuring his two daughters on his desk greeted me. The secretary closed the door. Stout did not offer me a seat. He wore a V-neck sweater vest with a white dress shirt underneath, the collar button undone.

I'm busy so make it quick, he said, regarding me with his thick-framed glasses. He had the severity of an old dean at a private college.

Sounds like you're too busy for the team then, I said, still standing.

Excuse me?

You heard me.

He dropped the pen he was holding, an expensive-looking fountain pen. It sounded hefty as it fell. There was an unsigned signature line below him.

Look, I don't know what your problem is, he said.

My problem is you can't hit a backhand volley.

What?

Yeah. Maybe if you work on it, I'll put you in the lineup next week.

I'm entitled to play as a member of the club.

Not when I'm captain.

Okay, hotshot. Why don't I see you at the club tomorrow afternoon then? I'll show you how it's done.

Good, I said. Show me.

I will.

But I want to watch you play, Dad, my son said, bleating from the back, boosted by his booster. I had told him no the first time.

I need to concentrate, I said.

I'll leave you alone, he said. I promise.

We were on the way to the club. I was gripping the steering wheel hard, my chest felt tight. I couldn't tolerate a break in the routine.

Can we just try once, please. Please!

Okay! I said. Now quiet!

At a stop light, I took a deep breath. When I looked in the rearview his eyes were there, looking right at me.

Here's the deal, I said, turning around. If I give you this opportunity, you need to be as silent as night when I'm on court. No talking unless I talk to you first, got it?

Got it.

There's more. If the ball goes over the fence, you're gonna shag it. If I need water, an extra towel, a banana, something from the pro shop, you're gonna get it. Got it?

He nodded in understanding.

The light's green, Dad—and that's how our new arrangement began.

When I arrived the following afternoon to play Stout, my son came with—we were on center court, next to the snack shop, the pool, and he sat courtside on one of the tall steps, holding opposite elbows with opposite hands. There was a ten-knot onshore breeze, not a cloud in the sky, a real summer day. The pool was packed. The breeze carried sunscreen scents—coconut, pineapple, key lime—and voices.

Stout had a big loopy two-hander and a nasty forehand slice. His game was unorthodox, better for singles than doubles, and he could disguise his forehand dropshot—it was real nice.

He gamed me though. What he did after our warm-up was suggest a baseline game to 11, a game that didn't allow for serving. Instead, the point was started with a hand feed. Every ball counted, including the feed.

So what good ol' Stout would do was feed a high ball and I'd have to take a few steps back unless I wanted to hit it on the rise, a low percentage shot, and by the time I returned the feed I was already almost against the back wall. From here, Stout, regardless, would run around his backhand and hit a drop shot. On occasion I could get there, but I almost pulled my hammy on one—I could feel a tightening, a clenching, and a tiny stab of pain from that region of my body.

Stout won the game 11–6.

How about we play a set with serves and returns.

Fine with me, Stout said.

Freddie, I said to my son. Get me a Gatorade, would you? Just give them our last name at the window. And like that, my son hopped to his feet and fetched me a cool bottle.

During the first changeover, I asked him for another towel and he disappeared inside the club and returned moments later with not one but two. I blew my nose in one and dabbed my forehead and eyebrows with the other.

Stout had difficulty with my out-wide serve on the deuce. I'd pull him off court and go to the opposite side with my next shot.

He moved well front and back but his lateral movement suffered. Sometimes, I'd follow the serve in and bunt an easy volley as he had the tendency of blocking the ball back high. However, I couldn't break him.

At 4–4 with Stout to serve, I waved my son over to my side of the court. Stout toweled off, then waited for me with his hands on his waist.

Son, I said, kneeling down next to him. Now don't look now, but there are a group of boys sitting at a high table next to the court over there. What I want you to do is go over there and play a game with them.

What game?

The game is called make-an-animal-noise.

Like Old-Macdonald-had-a-farm?

Kind of. But I want you to do it whenever you see the guy I'm playing against toss the ball up to serve. You got it?

Got it, Dad.

Okay, head on over. My son bolted off the court. Out of the corner of my eye, I could see him approach the group of three boys, towels wrapped around them, hair still wet from the pool.

Sorry about that, I said to Stout.

He wicked off more sweat from his forehead with a finger. Then, he approached the T and started to bounce the ball. I bent my knees, waiting in the ready position. I saw the ball leave his fingers as he began his motion to serve. Then, a cacophony of sounds. The ball went into the net. Stout looked behind him, the boys laughing, my son somewhere behind the pack of them unseen. Stout bounced the ball again—three, four times—tossed it eleven o'clock—and I heard a chirp, a bark, a squeak, and a growl. Double fault. 0–15. Stout turned and glared at the group and they were silent instantly. My son was back courtside now, a smart maneuver on his part to give the appearance that he wasn't complicit—he thought of this all on his own—and Stout pocketed one ball and bounced the other on the ad side. The ball went up, and a jungle erupted behind him.

Out! I called, his serve almost landing at my feet on the baseline. Stout quickly bounced the next ball and lobbed it up in the air, serving me a weaker than average second. I nailed it crosscourt. He stretched out his racquet, giving me an easy layup put-away, and I hit an overhead for the winner. 0–30. The tote-bearing mothers of the boys appeared on the stairs with wet hair, and the boys disappeared, but Stout looked stunned. At 0–30 he missed his first serve, and I was able to fend off his second—he hit a forehand just long. Then, at 0–40 he double-faulted, the phantom sounds from the boys still playing in his head. My son and I exchanged a smile. I broke to go up 5–4, and a game later with a soaked gray T-shirt, Stout met me at net, shaking his head. We shook hands.

Good set, I said.

Did you hear those little fuckers? Stout said.

Not in front of my son, please. I said.

I'm sure it's nothing he hasn't heard before. Stout shoved his racquet in his duffel, shouldered it, and shunted toward the glass door of the main building.

I'll release the lineup for the next match soon, I said, but Stout was gone.

Did I do good? my son said.

You did very good.

What are you having? I said.

A French martini.

I sat down next to her and ordered a Pisco sour. The far mirrored wall of the bar had the liquor, the stacked upside-down glasses, and the uplighting gave everything a fin-de-siècle, dramatic effect.

When do you want your lesson? I asked.

Her hair was down, wavy, just past her shoulders. Her eyebrows were tapered, arched, giving me the impression that I was being studied by an exotic Egyptian cat.

I met your son, she said.

Oh yeah?

The lady in childcare was chaperoning him for a snack at the snack bar. He came up to me, asked me my name. He's a confident young boy, she said. He asked me how I knew you.

What did you say?

I told him the truth. That we just met. Does your wife come to the club?

She isn't a member.

I looked for her left hand, her ring finger, but it was wrapped around the stem of her standing martini glass.

And you're married, I said, taking a guess.

Is that a question?

Happily married?

I'm married, she answered, raising her glass, taking a sip. I didn't see a ring on her finger.

You're here a lot, she said.

Does that bother you?

No, I like it, she said. Do you not work?

I'm in between gigs.

Not a bad way to spend it.

What about you?

I don't need to work, she said.

That must be nice.

Not because of my husband.

Oh, I said.

You still haven't told me how much you charge?

For what?

A lesson.

How serious are you?

From a small bowl, she stabbed a bright green olive with a toothpick, and before putting it in her mouth, she said, Let's keep it casual.

She lifted the olive wood bowl, held it out for me. With a little hesitation, I pinched one with my fingers. She watched me put it in my mouth.

It tasted surprisingly sweet.

Hi Ned, this is Carol with Omnivision. You had a virtual interview scheduled for today. There might have been a miscommunication. Um, either way, we're still interested if you want—

I deleted the voicemail.

It was a Sunday and the childcare wasn't open, my wife nowhere to be found.

It was 9:36 A.M. and I had a plan.

My players were practicing at the club, and I wanted to be there, needed to be there.

I couldn't risk another Target run for what I had in mind, another outburst in broad daylight from my son. So, I used Doordash instead, settling on a Dinosaur Lego set—a T-rex skull toy. I bought two of them.

On the bottom shelf of the pantry I found a gift bag. I found some blue tissue paper in the office. When the Doordash arrived, I placed one of the Lego packages in the bag and stuffed the tissue paper around it.

I told my son to take a piss.

I told my son to keep his clothes on from the day before.

I said we could skip the brushing of teeth, the combing of hair, that he could use some wipes to clean himself instead of a shower or a bath. I couldn't remember the last time he had one.

I grabbed a hat for myself. I chewed some spearmint gum. I zapped a slice of cheese pizza in the microwave and served it to him on a plate that I balanced on the roof of the car while I buckled him into his booster seat. I put his shoes on without socks. I told him we were going on an adventure.

The first park I drove by was uneventful. A private soccer lesson with two young brothers on the field, a ginger in the sandbox. I kept going.

The second park was bigger, more spread out, a maze of amenities. The park had a baseball field, a basketball court, a handball wall. It had two playgrounds—one for the big kids, one for the littles. It also had several grassy areas and a sunken concrete garden theater. There were picnic tables, a Power Ranger bounce house coming to life, being filled with air like a giant balloon. There were decorations, kids, an uncut cake, a picnic table covered in presents.

I pulled into a parking slot, put the car in park. I turned around to my son, handed him the gift bag with the present.

Look inside, I said, and he complied.

See that? That's a gift. Now here's the deal. We're going to walk over to that boy's birthday party and you're going to pretend you know him, that you go to his school. Got it?

What's in it for me? my son said, a little sparkle in his eyes.

You like that T-Rex Lego set?

My son nodded.

Want one?

Nodded again.

Well, I got one for you at home. And I'll give it to you. But only if you play along. Deal?

Deal.

As we approached the tables, the bounce house, the parents mingling, the kids chasing, the pizza delivery arriving, I skirted around until I found the cake.

Chester, it said, flanked by red-and-blue Power Rangers. *Happy 5th Birthday!*

I bent down.

The boy's name is Chester, I said into my son's ear.

He must be in kindergarten. So you're also in kindergarten.

No I'm not! I'm a first-grader, my son said, pulling away.

I grabbed his arm.

Not today you aren't. You want that present, right?

I stared into my son's eyes, leveled him. He nodded again.

Good. Now go play.

I was ready to introduce myself to the parents, to break into their circles, to sell ourselves. But after I placed our gift next to the other presents, I stood there for a second. There was a light breeze, only a few knots, and the leaves of the trees dangling happily, boys now bouncing in the bounce house including my son. Nothing else was needed on my part.

When I got back in the car, I didn't look back.

I found my men at the club, waiting for me like dutiful soldiers on Court #6. They let me lace up, jog around, stretch, and then we played some dingles.

It was a fine Sunday morning.

Sundays, as they say, are for the boys.

I had to circle the perimeter of the large park twice before finding a spot, a parallel parking job. I couldn't see the bounce house, and a little beeping noise, a panicking signal began to flare in my mind. It took me three tries to park the car. Someone honked and I gave them the finger. I looked over my shoulder. The back of my hair still wet from sweat sent a chill down my spine as I got out of the car. I jogged past the sunken theater to the plot of grass where I left my son. The bounce house was gone, the trash bins filled to the brim with pizza boxes and paper plates smeared with blue cake icing. There was a lone red balloon tied to the low branch of a tree.

I ran to one of the playgrounds, kids of all ages darting around, zigging and zagging, some with laser guns and backpacks, others with a kickball, scooters, and bikes, screams and cries and laughs and shouting, parents trailing, running after them, some seated on the bench eating grapes.

Freddie! I called. I looked for a head of blond hair. There were many, girls and boys, but none of them were him. I followed the concrete path to another field where a parent-run soccer game was underway, one team in red jerseys, the other team in plainclothes. There was another birthday party under a gazebo with a swaying pony piñata hanging from a tree nearby. On the baseball field, there was a boy hitting off a tee, and then on another soccer field, dogs were roaming unleashed, their owners looking on, lobbing tennis balls in the air for fetch. Blank windows of ranch-style houses and old condos and beach bungalows stared at me. Cars whooshed by, driving too fast. There was an ice-cream truck at the corner blaring its tinkle, drawing a crowd of cash-only carrying parents—fuck them, they were perfect. I kept running, going. I ran and ran until I found myself back at the original field near the red balloon. I punched it and screamed his name.

I grabbed my phone. I called my wife. Straight to voicemail.

I was back at a playground, but a different one. This one had four slides and a swing set, a climbable rocket ship. I turned round and round searching. I grabbed my phone and parked myself under a tree and called 911. I was breathing fast. My chest hurt. I needed to pee. I was sweating again. I was out of breath. The phone wasn't ringing and I realized it was because I hadn't pressed call, but when I looked at the screen it was my wife.

Accept or Decline, the phone screen prompted me, and when I pressed Accept it was too late, my voicemail had picked up the call.

I felt nauseous, sick. The ice-cream truck had pulled up to the red-painted part of the curb, kids were running over, the high-pitched song seemingly screeching.

I saw a stooped-over mom walking an unridden tricycle. I drew up a photo of my son on my phone.

I placed the phone under her nose.

Have you seen my son? Have you seen him?

She shook her head, pointed in the general direction of the playground, other adults with arms crossed looking on.

I called my son's name. I asked other parents. I looked up at the sky.

My son, my son!

And then I felt something at my leg, tugging the pocket of my pants.

Dad, do you have any money for the ice-cream truck?

I got down on my knees and embraced him. Then I grabbed his shoulders and studied his face, his clothes.

It was my son indeed. He was my son, and he was fine. I held him by the shoulders.

Where did you go? I said. I said it again sternly, held him firm, like it was his fault.

Dad, you're hurting me, he said.

I loosened my grip.

Don't do that again, I said. Okay?

Don't do what, Dad?

I grabbed his hand and marched him to the car.

Don't do what?

Hot tears were running down my face. I banished them with the hair on my forearm and I drove my son to Jack in the Box, where I got him an Oreo milkshake.

Regular or large? the voice of a woman asked.

Large, I said to the speaker.

I parked the car by the ocean while the sun was setting, my son sucking on the straw.

He drank every last drop.

He deserved it.

The match was a week and half away, and still no Roland. Bray was out, but Stout was in. With Thiago evicted, I was short on guys. I needed Roland, otherwise we would have to default a line.

First, I called the club and asked for Ken.

When's the last time Roland was at the club?

Let me check with the front desk, Ken said.

A minute went by.

He hasn't been here since last Sunday.

The day of our match.

Correct, Ken said.

I was overlooking center, no one on it, the hot air still. It was middle of the day, the club nearly empty. I heard the light splashes of the water fountain, a ball being struck on a far court.

I felt a tap on my shoulder followed by a breeze. I smelled lavender as she passed, hair swept back, an orange tennis dress strapped to her shoulders.

She gave a little wave.

Court 5, she said.

I followed her. The hem of her dress ended a little more than halfway down her thighs, and I lost sight of her as she turned a corner behind one of the green windscreens of a court.

When I reached Court 5, I mounted the three steps and closed the gate behind me.

There was a basket of balls at the service line, untouched. Her back was to me, her fingers working her hair into a ponytail, followed by the donning of a visor. I set my bag down near her feet, her white tennis shoes, not a mark on them.

Turning to me suddenly, she asked, What are we doing today, coach?

What do you need to work on?

I was hoping you could look at everything.

We stood on opposite sides of the net. Mini tennis. I hit the ball gently to her. She took it seriously. She bounced, split-stepped, guided with her left hand when she hit a forehand. Eventually we moved back to the baseline.

Sorry, I said, mishitting a ball into a corner of the court, but she tracked it down.

Don't apologize, she said after.

During our water break, she didn't sit. I watched the rise and fall of her chest in between sips. I watched a tiny bead of sweat roll down her neck. I wanted to meet it with the tip of my finger.

Do you think you could look at my serve next?

I joined her near the baseline. I stood the basket up, kicking each of its legs into place. There was no one around us.

I tossed her balls from the alley, one at a time, as she threw them up in the air and chased after them with her racquet as she served.

Looking good, I said.

Don't be nice, she said.

Okay, I said. Bend your knees a little more, I said.

She tried again.

Better, I said.

I watched her bare tan arm tense during the next serve.

Relax your arm, I said.

I don't know how to.

Try again.

She did.

Show me.

I stepped up to her.

Here. Hold my hand.

I stuck mine out.

She gripped it. Her hand felt cool, her fingers soft.

Your hand is so much bigger than mine, she said.

Feel my grip, I said. Feel how loose it is?

I see, she said.

That's how you should grip your racquet, I said. I could feel a swelling coming on. I started to pull away.

Wait, let me try, she said, grasping me.

How's that?

A little hard, I said.

How about that? She was looking right at me.

Better, I said.

And this? She looked down, then up again. She smiled. I could see her white teeth.

Just right, I said.

Her hand was still in mine. She was right there, in front of me.

At the corner of my eye, something shifted, a blur.

I let go.

A father and son stepped onto the court right next to us. The father waved to me. He was carrying a basket of balls. His son was around my son's age.

Time's up I guess, she said. She was already walking over to her bag, bending down, holstering her racquet.

The way she had looked at me—I hadn't been looked at that way in a long time.

The next day, I received an email from the organization:

Dear Captains,

There has been a late season entry. Fair Oaks Country Club has submitted a team. Please check your schedules accordingly.

Captain Maddock was included in the email, and the following weekend, my team was slated to play Fair Oaks.

Fair Oaks was in the upper part of town—a true country club with a lofty initiation fee, a golf course, a waiting list, a society of its own. These were the kinds of families you wanted to be around. You were buying into a lifestyle, a culture. I didn't recognize any names on their roster.

I let the valet take my car, and I met my players through the double doors at the front desk.

We submitted our driver's licenses. We signed a waiver. A member scooted ahead of me, rattling off the four digits of his membership. He wore a golfer's hat, a sweater vest, and over the shoulder carried a bag full of clubs with heads of polished wood.

Ten twenty-three, he said.

That was the day before my birthday, 10/24.

We walked down the stairs. To our left was a gym with cardio machines as silent as electric cars, and to our right was a pro shop with electric stringing machines and high-end athletic wear. There was an office door for an in-house chiropractor, another one for a masseuse. Outside there was a grand view of the sunken center court, a true stadium court, flanked by other courts, trees, the golf course beyond. It was a kind of paradise. The air smelled different, better.

I initially had Bray in singles, Burris and myself at the one line in doubles, Stout and Snider at two. When I announced it via text the night before, everyone confirmed.

Stout, in a white visor, approached me.

Stacking us at the two line, Stout now said to me, overlooking the grounds.

Sure, I said. That's right. I stroked his ego. He needed to feel better than me, but we both knew the truth.

Then, a man I recognized with blond gelled hair with a nice little wave in the front, whitened teeth, blue eyes approached me. He was decked out in a dark blue polo and matching blue shorts, white tennis shoes. The polo was a little tight around his tummy. I saw a little paunch.

You're Ned, right?

Yes, I said.

I'm Stefan. Remember me?

Stefan, I thought to myself. The mullet. The academy. The competitor. The cheater.

Of course, I said. How could I ever forget you.

Looks like we're playing you today.

You're playing?

Yeah, I just rostered last night. Been playing much?

Oh you know, here and there.

Listen, our captain couldn't make it, so I have our lineup today. Stefan read it off, and my ears only heard the fact that he was playing singles.

I read off my roster.

Then I huddled my players around the water dispenser where empty pitchers stood stacked.

Listen, change of plans, I said. Burris, Stout, Snider, Bray—they all looked at me intently.

I'm playing singles now. Bray, you're taking my spot and playing with Burris. Stout and Snider, you're still at two.

What! Bray said. His mouth was open. I could see his bottom crooked front teeth.

This is a gametime decision.

Bullshit, Bray said. I'm playing singles.

No, I said calmly. You are not.

I am the captain and I decide, I said.

I haven't played doubles all week, Bray said.

Bray's right, Burris said.

Listen to the captain, Stout said.

Bray and Burris, you're on Court 2. Stout and Snider, Court 3.

I grabbed a pitcher and shoveled ice from the ice machine. Then, I filled it up with water, the ice crackling.

You're fucking up the whole season, Bray said in my face.

Focus on the W, I said to Bray. You'll get your shot at singles. I elbowed past him to center court.

When I set foot on the court, there was one spectator, an older gentleman in a green rugby shirt, khaki shorts, New Balance shoes, calf-high white socks. I recognized him immediately. It was Stefan's father.

Your dad calling lines for us?

Ha, Stefan said as he cracked open the can. So what do you do these days?

I'm in between gigs.

That must be nice. Married?

Yes.

Wife work?

She does.

Nice. Kids?

One boy. You?

Four. All boys. My little army.

They must keep you busy.

You got that right, he said. Shall we spin, get it over with?

Go.

Call it.

Up, I said.

His racquet landed face down on the court after the spin. The father was leaning forward, elbows on his knees.

It's down. I'll receive.

Confident choice.

I like to break early.

We'll see about that, pal.

We warmed up quickly. He hit a good ball still—penetrating ground strokes, classically trained. He had a good thorough follow-through on both sides, nice knee bend. He stepped into the ball each time. His movement though. That was his weakness.

Ready? he said.

I grabbed another sip of my electrolytes. I bit on my protein bar.

Ready, I said.

The match began.

I held my serve.

Then, he held his.

We went back and forth like this for a while, me edging closer to breaking each time.

At 3–3, I had my shot.

It was deuce.

He hit a serve out wide, and I rifled a forehand up the line. He barely got to it in time, popping it up for an easy put-away. I ran to the net as the ball hung in the air, and instead of popping a forehand volley into the open court, I decided to go behind him, up the line, and that's what I did. He was already barreling to the open court, his white tennis shoes squeaking in desperation. He couldn't change direction in time. Winner.

I fist-pumped.

Break point.

Out! I heard behind me. I turned. He was pointing at the alley.

The ball was out.

What?

Yep, he said, stomping over to a mark on the court, not mine, just outside the line.

That's not where it hit. I hit it inside the line. That's an older mark you're pointing at.

I looked at the father. He was shaking his head no, that I was wrong.

I saw it out too, the father said.

You, I said, can shut the fuck up.

Don't talk to my father that way, Stefan said, approaching the net.

Some things never change, huh, Stefan? Once a cheater, always a cheater.

It's my call, and I'm saying it was out.

Is that how you get ahead in life too? By cheating?

My face felt hot. I slammed the net with my racquet.

Bullshit, I said. Fucking bullshit.

Calm down, he said. We have rules here.

I took a deep breath. If I had wanted to, I could have reached across the net, grabbed him by the throat. If I had wanted to, I could have slammed my racquet into the side of his head.

Okay, I said.

I walked back to the baseline. Ready to return.

He bounced once, twice, three times, toss. Boom. The serve went down the T. I couldn't reach it. It landed on the line, but fuck him, I thought. Fuck this guy.

Out! I yelled.

What!?

Yeah, it was wide. I ran to the service box, pointed at a distinct mark.

His father was standing.

You're a liar and you know it, Stefan said.

The ball was out. My call, buddy.

You got a bad attitude, he said, walking away.

No, you have a bad fucking attitude, I said. I picked up the ball, hit it at him. It caught him by surprise—he jumped—but it didn't hit him.

You want to get kicked out? I'll get you thrown out of here so fast you'll need an ambulance to take you home.

Oh, is that right?

Just shut up and play tennis, you big baby.

I was under his skin. I was waiting to return. He bounced the ball once, twice, three times, four, tossed it. In the net. Double fault.

I went on to break serve, and then I held serve for the first set. I hit an overhead smash for the winning shot.

Yeah! I yelled. I fist-pumped, looked at the father, the son. I didn't sit down at the changeover. Standing, I drank my Gatorade, ate another bite of my protein bar.

The second set, Stefan had another strategy. He started hitting high deep balls, moon balls I liked to call it, the tactic of many ten-, eleven-, and twelve-year-old boys who are too scared to lose. I was no longer a boy though. I was a man. I knew what to do. I bided my time, waited for the right opportunity. Then, I'd rush the net and punch a volley to the open court. Stefan's father had left at this point, and I was up 2–0 with an early lead.

Then, at love-30 the next game, Stefan serving, I hit a nasty backspin dropshot mid-rally. Stefan tried to bolt for it, but his legs couldn't match his desire for the ball. He took a big heavy stride forward and then fell to the ground. He was clutching his thigh, on his back, his feet in the air. He looked like a bee that couldn't upright himself, legs kicking toward the sky. I let him struggle. I watched him from the other side of the net.

Eventually, he got himself up and hobbled over to his bag. He shoved his racquet in, and lumbered off the court, leaving his water behind, his towel, the balls scattered. He retreated to the shadow of the main building and entered. Minutes went by when he finally emerged again at a courtside table, his upper-right thigh wrapped in ice.

I had won. I had defeated my childhood nemesis.

I remained on center. I was marking my territory by staying in the arena. I was a gladiator, the last man standing.

The rest of my players, that was a different story.

We lost the match overall.

But I—I was still the victor.

It was that late in the daylight—warm, soft, vague shadows. The hanging pendant lights above the bar were on, and there were small lit candles near the garnish trays filled with wedges of lemon and lime, green olives. In front of me was a pint of Mexican lager. In front of Thiago, an IPA of some kind. I was still sweaty. Thiago, he looked dry with both elbows on the counter, shoulders slightly slumped. He hardly looked like the ringer that he was. More like a nine-to-fiver.

Drinks on me, he had said as I was bagging things up, after he kicked my ass in five super tiebreakers in a row. So now we were here, sitting on stools.

The lager was quenching, and I took another big gulp of it from the frosty mug.

How's married life? he said. Woah, you okay?

Wrong pipe, I said, pointing at my throat.

Thiago gave my back a gentle whack.

That bad, huh?

It's fine. Ebbs and flows.

You don't sound too excited. I haven't met your better half, but it seems like you got a good life, bud.

I'm just nursing my wounds still from the court. What about you? You spoken for yet?

Nope. No sir.

Must be nice. That freedom.

Yeah, he said, taking a drink of his own. I think I'm ready for a different set of problems though.

What, like credit card debt, mortgage, interrupted sleep until your kids go to college?

You're really selling me on it.

Just take your time, I said.

I was seated at the edge of the bar, and I looked out one of the long vertical windows. Down below, next to center, four women were playing doubles. One of them was Carlin. She was at the net, and I watched her in a volley exchange.

What you looking at over there?

I watched Carlin give a skip and a high-five to her partner after winning the point. Her white skirt fluttered a little.

Some talent over there?

You could say that.

There was a wedge of lime straddling the rim of my glass. I squeezed it a little, then pushed it over the edge into the beer.

Nothing wrong with looking at the menu, but keep it on the menu, buddy. I felt Thiago's heavy hand land on my shoulder.

I took another drink of my beer.

You gonna keep me out of trouble?

I will if I have to, he said.

I was out by the lawn closest to Court 3, the lawn with the gazebo. I stood outside of it, the white gazebo, and my hands held the rails as I had one foot forward, one foot back, stretching a calf.

You trying to tip that thing over? Ken said sauntering.

Huh?

It looks like you're trying to push the gazebo with your Herculean strength.

Ah, I said, switching feet to stretch the left calf now.

Free to talk for a sec?

I have a ladder match in twenty minutes.

Against who?

Garth, I said.

Garth Garner?

Yeah, that's him.

Oh, you'll smoke him, Ken said, waving a hand in front of his nose like he was trying to clear a bad odor. He wore a two-button polo. The polo was navy blue, fitted, and his chinos were the color of midnight. There was something on his mind, I could tell.

What did you want to talk about?

The team, he said, letting out a big breath, his chest sinking.

What about it?

Tough loss last weekend, I heard.

It happens.

Listen, I'm just going to come out and say it. You are the captain, but you are also leading a team of fellow members.

I pushed away from the gazebo. I couldn't tell if Ken's eyes were wet or if it was the light, the low sun making them appear moist.

Is this a coup?

It's not a coup, but I've listened to several of your players lobby complaints. And with last week's loss, your record as captain has a blemish now.

So it's a coup.

No, Ken said putting a firm flat hand up in the air as if to say *halt*, like he was directing traffic.

I want you to run the lineup by me from now on, Ken said pausing. A collaboration, he said.

There were some pesky hummingbirds above us. They were buzzing around. I wanted to dig out the dead ball in the soil of the weeping ficus planter and hit them with it.

My job is to keep the members happy, Ken continued.

What about me, I said. My happiness.

Your happiness is important to me too, Ken said.

But, I said.

But, Ken continued. You are only one member.

My son is on my membership.

He doesn't really count, Ken said.

He could be a great player one day though, I said. Make this club look good.

My son, he hated tennis.

I'm sure he is already a fine player with a great tennis-playing father like you.

On the path up ahead, a man with floppy blond hair waved and called. I glanced behind me, then back at the man.

Oh, that's Garth, Ken said.

I must have looked unimpressed because the next thing Ken said was repeating the refrain—I told you, you'll smoke him.

Garth was closer now, taller than he appeared from a distance. He was stalky, strong, dressed in all white—polo, shorts, shoes, socks, a wrist band on his right wrist—and he shook my hand with a strong grip, leaving a lingering knuckle pain as he released me.

Pleasure, he said.

Nice to meet you, I said, as I rubbed my sore hand with my other one.

Well, I'll let you boys get to it. Have a great match, gentleman, Ken said.

And Ned, he winked. We'll talk.

I followed Garth to Court 4. He had balls, a can of Völkls, heavier than bricks.

He hit a real flat ball in the warm-up, and I shanked one onto the street behind us when returning his serve in the first game.

I lost the set, then the match.

I couldn't stop thinking about my conversation with Ken.

My son was on his knees, the toilet seat up. He puked silently. All I heard was the aftermath—the splash.

I looked at my watch. I was ten minutes late.

We gotta go!

Dad! my son said, gasping. I can't!

I'll buy you a Gatorade, I said. The blue one you like.

Dad, I'm sick.

His head disappeared into the bowl. I heard another splash.

Okay, I said. Okay.

I called from my phone. On the second ring, a voice answered.

Can I leave a message for someone?

Sure, the front desk girl said. First name and last name?

Her name is Carlin. I don't know her last name. We were supposed to hit today. Tell her I'm sorry, that I'll make it up to her. Promise. An emergency.

I caught a whiff of myself, the new cologne I had sprayed on moments ago.

Burris sent me the video, the link.

Found it on Reddit, he wrote.

The video was handheld, taken from a phone. In the foreground was a sandbox, a slide, a set of horse seesaws. A dirty blonde child with pigtails ran across the screen. Then the camera started to zoom, and that's when the tennis court became visible. Just outside the green chain-link fence was a man I did not recognize holding a clipboard, and then another man, a man with a visor and a beard—it was Maddock—mid-argument. There was a third party, a sweating player on the court, arms akimbo, taking it all in. The man arguing with Maddock appeared to be the captain of the other team. I could hear their muffled words on the video.

The ball was in by a mile!

You can't overrule the call. You're not an official, and you're not playing the match.

I was standing right there. Your player hooked mine.

It's my guy's call. I can pull up the rulebook if you'd like, Maddock said.

The camera started shaking, the person filming moving closer.

The other captain stepped forward, arm's distance from Maddock, and stepped forward again, kissing distance from Maddock.

Don't tell me what I can and can't do.

Maddock held his ground.

Want me to call an official? I can call an official.

Sure, you little bitch.

You're out of line, pal. Back off or I'll get your ass disqualified.

The man, the other captain in a striped polo, seemed to take this in stride. He backed off a little, still in arm's reach, looking down to the ground, weighing his options. His barrel chest heaved underneath the cloth. He lowered his shaved head even more like he was about to bend his knees before an altar. The camera was dead still, the playground around nearly silent. This moment seemed to last forever.

Then, it happened. The collision. The camera jolted forward as the man used his head as a battering ram right into Maddock's solar plexus. Maddock thudded to the ground like a fallen tree, and a scream from the park echoed behind camera, a child, a witness. The player on the court came to Maddock's aid while the camera still trained on the head butter before dropping and all we could see was pavement and weeds in the cracks.

Dear Captains,

Due to unforeseen circumstances, the Fair Oaks team has forfeited the rest of the season. Please check your team schedule accordingly.

The Organization

There were only two teams left: mine and Maddock's.

It was my fifth lesson with Joachim, and he meant business.

Let's see if I still got it, kid.

He opened two cans of balls. He was in a sleeveless tee. He had zinc oxide painted on the bridge of his nose. He jumped high into the air, tucking his knees into his chest. He did this twice. He looked like a grasshopper.

I spun my racquet, and he won the toss. The toss, however, was the only thing he won. I kicked my coach's ass in thirty minutes.

Out of breath, he sat down on the plastic bench and reached into his bag. When he removed his hand from the depths, he was holding a pack of cigarettes. He pulled one out, lit it up with a cheap lighter, took a few puffs. He blew smoke out of the side of his mouth, and the tiny cloud wafted over in my direction.

Holy shit, man, he said. How old are you again?

39, I told him.

Still some good years left in the engine. You could make a run for it.

A run for it?

On tour, he said.

I laughed.

Really? I said.

Oh yeah!

After I slipped my racquet into my bag, Joachim charged me the full hour.

I found Roland's home address through my team roster.

The first thing I noticed about the house was the piece of cardboard like an eye patch covering a hole just below the roof. The roof itself dipped at the center, and the exterior of the house looked rotted. The wooden steps bowed and creaked like I was on an old bridge about to give. The yard itself had an expelled look to it—brown and yellow with wild green weeds, the color of vomit. The door was open, opening into the living room. An old box TV sat crooked on a desk in the middle of the room, and in front of it was a La-Z-Boy chair half covered in a brown blanket. There was a plastic plate upright and leaning against the foot of the chair. The carpeted floor was maroon, and the walls looked like they used to be white. At the corner of one, starting from the base on both sides, black mold crawled up like a Rorschach resembling a large spread-winged bat. The air had a heavy, humid quality to it—it was hard to breath.

Hello? I called again.

I'm not interested in what you're selling, a voice croaked.

I'm not selling anything, I replied, still standing just inside the door.

From around the corner came Vernon wheeling. One of the wheels was bent. When Vernon's wife died, he turned to alcohol, and he never recovered. The damage he had done was irreversible. He could manage with a cane, but after a bad fall that resulted in a broken femur, he was forced into a wheelchair. This is what I had learned since his appearance at our recent match.

There were empty cans of Keystone all over the floor.

What do you want? His eyes caught a slant of sunlight coming through the front doorway as he approached. The white of his eyes looked yellow as if filled with rusty water. His green irises looked gray.

I'm looking for Roland.

His van is here, but he isn't.

Do you know where he is?

No.

Have you talked to him since the match?

Haven't seen him since. Had to call an Uber home. He was my ride back.

You sure were talking a lot to him during the match.

Old wounds. I couldn't help but scratch.

Maybe that's why he left, I said.

If he didn't want the unvarnished truth, he shouldn't have invited me to the match.

With a strong grip, he maneuvered his wheels, spinning over an already crushed can until he faced the TV. With the remote, he turned it on. It came on static and too loud. He rolled forward, slapped the side of it hard. The TV, it seemed to listen. A baseball game was on. The announcers were shouting. I asked if he could turn it down. He did.

Is Roland in trouble? he said.

It depends on how you define trouble.

Are the cops looking for him?

No.

Well then, he's not in trouble.

I figured they'd can his ass. What's he to you?

I grew up with him.

He looked at me hard. His face had a beard rash. He looked swollen.

I said, Do you have a recent photo you could lend me?

He kept looking at me, then with a jerk, wheeled himself forward into the kitchen. There were pots and pans on the linoleum, and the window above the sink was draped with old curtains, the light coming in gauzed. He reached in a drawer and pulled out a stack and spread them on the metal kitchen table next to a small plate where an old half-eaten apple sat.

There were photos of Roland playing tennis, holding trophies, one next to his dad, Vernon's big arm around him proud. There was one of Roland and his younger sister, the early high-school years, the proud older brother, the giddy sister—she loved him so much. Then, there was a photo of her holding a baby, another child standing at her waist, and a man with glasses, all in formal attire, under a tree with pink flowers.

She sends me a postcard every year. From Kansas.

Now, he was looking down at the photo of his once-young son hoisting a trophy. Roland was smiling like he was at Disneyland.

His father took that photo—Vernon was behind the camera. Roland was smiling at his father.

In the middle of the fanned-out stack he plucked one—a photo of Roland with his hair a little longer, the curled locks coming in. He was in a room, the photo taken from a close angle, the light yellow.

One of his girlfriends took this of him. She was nice. Sometime after his sentence.

He handed it to me. Then, he gathered the rest into a pile with both hands swiftly like a dealer in a casino and shoved them back into the drawer from where they came. He slammed the drawer shut and reached for the fridge. He popped a can. It sounded like a small gun.

I followed him down the hall where the backdoor opened to a DIY wood ramp. The backdoor, I noticed, was unlocked. He rolled down the ramp.

The backyard didn't look much better than the front of the house, and he wheeled himself over to a yellow garage with chipped paint—it looked like a barn, the wood rotted. He gestured to the pulley—a weathered rope—and I lifted the tilt-door. I stood back. Inside was a small twin bed, the frame natural wood, probably IKEA.

There was a stack of books, a stepladder as bedside table with a lamp without a lampshade, just the bulb. There was a pair of jeans, a hoodie, some T-shirts, and a Carhartt jacket hanging from black steel pipes mounted to one of the walls. On the ground was a pair of old tennis shoes, the sole splitting apart, the tongue missing from one.

He liked to fish, didn't he? I suddenly remembered.

Oh yeah. He'd clean his catches sometimes right here in the backyard on the grass, guts all over the place. But when he cooked it, it tasted real good.

I looked around.

I don't see a fishing rod anywhere, I said.

I don't see it either. Maybe he took it with him to Hawaii, Vernon said, wheeling back, laughing.

On my way out, I told him I'd let him know if I found him. I'd bring back the photo.

You can keep it, he said.

He turned up the volume as a player hit a foul ball.

Roland must have come home after the match. His car was there.

I tried to think of all the places he might go from there.

I turned the dial for the jets all the way up. I was dripping wet. She was waiting for me. I caught her glance as I walked back. She was taking me in from the water, her arms resting on either side of the jacuzzi's brim. I saw the steam rise around her, the water bubbling, frizzing, like freshly poured champagne. Her eyes met mine. Her one-piece had a deep plunge at the neckline. She smiled. Her hair was dry, tied in a bun, and her diamond stud earrings sparkled a little from the underwater jacuzzi lights. I stepped back into the hot water, and I positioned myself catty corner from her. I sat with a strong jet massaging my lower back. I stretched my legs out a little, and her foot grazed mine. She kept it there.

So is your son feeling better?

He is, I said.

And he's in the childcare right now.

I nodded.

So you get some alone time. The bottom of her foot stroked the top of mine. Must be nice, she said.

Yes, I said. They close in about thirty minutes though.

The sky was darkening, the palm trees looming like dark shadows.

So, where do you see this going, Ned? Her foot stopped moving, and I felt the weight of it all of the sudden.

I don't know, I said. What about you?

I think it would be nice to get together outside of the club.

I didn't respond.

Don't you? she asked.

That might be difficult, I said.

My son, I said.

A pair of tall wiry legs descended. The body belonged to an older swimmer in a speedo. Carlin's foot retreated from mine. I felt the grit on the bottom of the jacuzzi with my heel. It needed to be cleaned.

Mind if I join?

Please do, Carlin said.

I watched the man sink back against the wall, dipping his body into the roiling water so only chin and above were exposed. His head titled back a little and his eyes closed. His lips were slightly parted. He groaned.

I'm getting hot, Carlin announced.

Leaving the party already? the man said to her.

I'm afraid so.

I watched her ascend the stairs. She wrapped one towel under her arms and picked up her sandals. She walked away barefoot without even a wave. I let her.

The man groaned again. He was nudging himself against one of the jets. His foot touched mine.

Pretty friend you got there, the man said.

You got something to write with?

I don't, I said to Ken over the phone.

You might want to grab a pen.

I think I can remember the lineup.

I'd prefer if you write it down.

Why don't you email me then?

I'd prefer not to have this in writing.

That's very interesting, Ken.

Now now, Ned. Let's play nice.

I had a tennis ball in my hand. I was bouncing it against the wall in our living room. I threw it hard just under a framed photo of my wife and me on our wedding day. The frame was a little crooked now. I left it that way.

Dad, stop, my son said. I'm trying to concentrate. He was playing a game on his iPad on the couch.

I'm ready, I said to Ken.

He gave me the lineup. I didn't hear a word he said.

Got it, I said.

You got it?

I got it.

Repeat it back to me, Ken said.

I hung up the phone.

On Friday morning, I texted the team my lineup.

Saturday morning, early. Twenty-seven hours before our next match. I had just made myself a pour-over, my son and wife still sleeping, when the name *Stout* appeared on the face of my phone. 7:13 A.M.

Hello?

Ned, it's Stout. I'm in bad health. I've been puking all night.

What happened?

Food poisoning.

I need you for the match tomorrow.

I don't think I can play.

I understand that, but the team needs you.

It's coming out of both ends.

Try to rest and recover.

The fuck you think I'm doing?

I can bring you something.

I have a wife, Stout said.

Where were you poisoned?

The Drunken Clam.

Never been, I said. I heard him cough. It sounded like a gag.

You okay?

Yeah, he said. And that other captain was there seated a few tables over.

Maddock?

Yeah, him.

I meditated on this. Maddock. Maddock, the other captain. The veteran captain. What was he doing at the same restaurant?

Did he arrive before you or after you? I said.

After, he said. He was waiting for someone, he added.

A lone wolf. Who were you with? I asked.

With my family, of course.

Did Maddock say hello to you?

No.

Did you guys make eye contact?

No.

Did you ever leave the table unattended?

A pause.

I went to use the bathroom once, and my wife went with one of our girls.

At the same time?

Sure.

Did your other daughter remain at the table?

Well, no. They're both under six.

I understand, I said.

I said, So just to clarify, the whole family went to the bathroom?

Yes. It was a family affair.

Was your food on the table at this point?

It had just arrived.

What did you order?

Are you trying to make me sick?

What?

I don't want to talk about food.

This is important.

I ordered the sea bass.

Did you have a drink with it?

I had a Gin basil smash. Two of them. Want to know what color underwear I was wearing?

That's not necessary.

I'm going to hang up now.

Rest up, I said.

Fuck you, he said.

Maddock. He must have poisoned Stout. I knew it sounded crazy, but I was convinced. By process of elimination, he probably determined that Stout would be in the lineup for our next match. He must have followed Stout from his house to the restaurant with some coolant, some antifreeze. I suspected he used a dropper—one of those glass dropper bottles. He used the dropper on the sea-bass soy glaze. I looked at the menu.

First, he blocked Thiago, and now he poisoned my player. At first, I suspected he even tipped off Vernon about Roland's match appearance. Maddock. Maddock was arsenic to the whole league.

It was Saturday morning, and my wife was home, so I could rely on her for childcare. In fact, since she had been working all week, she needed to spend some quality time with our son.

A quick internet search gave me Maddock's home address.

He lived on a street called Drapery Lane. I drove over. It was a quiet one-way street. He lived in a small cottage right where the road dipped. I parked on higher ground, across the street, and watched the front door. It was 8:30 A.M.

The front door was painted red. The windows were painted blue. The house itself, the facade, was all white. There was a flag holder mounted between one of the windows with no flag.

At 9:07, the front door opened, and a buzz-cut man in a tank top, flip-flops, and shorts appeared, rubbing his eyes with one hand, holding a brown mug with the other. I suspected that this was Maddock's roommate. The roommate disappeared inside, the front door shut.

At 9:35, the front door opened again and this time it was Maddock. He was in a baseball cap and basketball shorts and a hoodie. He closed the door but didn't lock it. His first mistake.

Maddock, you think you're such a veteran, but I'll get you, I promised myself as he got into the driver's seat of a green Jeep.

His first stop was the bank. He didn't go inside, but got cash from the ATM outside. Maybe payoff money. 9:57.

The next stop was Dick's sporting goods. I parked next to the Whole Foods. At 10:25 he emerged with two arms full of Penn tennis ball cans. When he tried to lift open the truck, they fell to the asphalt.

I followed him to Costco, and at 11:04 he emerged with a cart full of Gatorade, the red kind, and cases of water. They went into his trunk.

At 11:18, my wife called, but I didn't answer.

11:47—back at Drapery Lane. Maddock slotted into the only available street parking spot. I drove past hoping he didn't see me. I circled the block for five minutes and found another spot that freed up at the top of the street, the Jeep still there.

12:25, my wife texted me: *When are you coming home? Celeste wants to go for a walk with me.*

12:53, Maddock emerged from the house in a pair of jeans and no hat, showered.

1:01 at a red light, my car inevitably pulled alongside his. I stayed a few meters ahead. With a sandalwood comb, Maddock combed his red neck beard, presumably plotting his next move against my team.

At 1:20, I followed his Jeep into the restaurant parking lot of Nineteen-Eighty Flour. I remained in the car. The restaurant was all glass, and I saw him seat himself at one of the window booths. At 1:25, a silver sedan parked alongside me, and a woman in a blouse got out. The woman looked familiar, like I had seen her before. Her face was puffy, and she wore her hair in a lazy plait bundled in the back. This woman, I knew her, I told myself. I had seen her, and my eyes followed her. She opened one of the heavy wooden double doors of the restaurant and lo and behold sat across from Maddock. There was no hug or greeting, she simply sat down across from him—Maddock and this woman I somehow knew. I raised my phone and zoomed in and took a picture. Their faces were makeable but blurry. I needed a better shot, but I didn't want to draw attention to myself either. I noticed a closer parking spot, so I reversed the car.

In the new spot, there was glare in the glass. I took a photo, but the glare, it blocked the shot, their faces, even when I tried a filter, when I played with the exposure.

I had a pile of used surgical masks stuffed at the bottom of the center console. I put one on my face—it smelled like coffee.

I went inside the restaurant and the headwaiter and attendants were busy with another party, so I skirted along. There were booths and a counter, and a display section of cakes. There were the bathrooms down the hall. On the way to the bathrooms was Maddock and this woman I somehow knew, seated with ice water, deep in conversation. I would do a drive-by shot, I decided. I would walk by with my phone raised to my hip and catch Maddock with this woman. It was coming together. I raised my phone as I approached, Maddock with his neckbeard, and I rapid fired a few shots. In the stall of the floor-to-ceiling black-tiled bathroom, I reviewed my work. I only had a clear shot of Maddock, the woman more or less in profile. On the way out, I would need another. My phone buzzed. My wife was calling again.

I left the stall and washed my hands. Someone in Crocs was in another stall.

Back in the restaurant, I raised my phone and took some clearer shots as I bumped into someone. A waitress. A tray had fallen—something shattered. I stared down at three cherries floating in mounds of vanilla and chocolate and broken glass, the remnants of milkshakes. I heard a child cry.

I'm so sorry, I said to the waitress. Patrons were looking at me, my back to Maddock and the woman, and I rushed to the front door. I heard commotion, voices behind me, and I got outside and made a lap around the block before returning to my car. Then, I noticed something. On the rear windshield of the car that belonged to the woman, there was a car sticker advertising the tennis organization. On the way home, I called my wife.

How's your day going, honey?

The woman that Maddock was with was Holly Goonis. The car decal gave it away. I found her on the organization's website, her picture—in her headshot she wore a scarf, but her face, it was distinct, it was clear. I compared the photo from the restaurant with the photo on the website. It was the same person. She was the director of the region. The director of the region was having lunch with the captain of the other team.

This whole league was an inside job, and Maddock had an inside track.

I had the evidence that I needed.

Maddock was fucked.

I could hear her moaning on the other side of the door. I listened. At first, I thought she might be hurt. But the moaning continued with two- to three-second periods between. The shower was running. I stayed there at the door. Then, gently, I grabbed the knob and turned it softly. The door made a sound as it pushed against the air, but she didn't hear it. Steam hit my face. I pushed the door open a little farther and my wife was in the shower alone behind the fogged-up glass, her back to me blurry. She was on her tippy toes with one foot, the other foot flat on the pebbled ground, and one of her arms was crooked and bent, her hand at work in between her legs. I stood there as she moaned again, my hand still holding the knob, a little tighter now. I stood there and watched.

Then, I closed the door quietly and went downstairs.

Why are you doing that? Luke asked me. Luke was my teammate. He was the #1 player on the team—full ride. I was on a partial. Peanuts. Hardly anything—30k in loans just for one year.

I was running every day. On the track, in the gym, at the beach, on the sand. I needed to get ahead. I was #4 in the lineup. Coach Palmer promised if I cracked the top 3 by end of season, he could get me 75 percent the following year.

Jeremie, one of the Frenchmen, had seen me running on the track behind the baseball field. He had ratted me out to the others. They were nervous. They were scared. I was coming for them. I was coming for Luke. He could feel it.

My teammates, they were smoking every day. European. Their lungs—they'd get a little heavy. Running was my edge.

Luke was the only other American on the team. The coach had a direct pipeline to France and Spain. He had connections to the academies out there. He had scouts. I was basically a walk-on, and Luke was his big non-Euro recruit from Texas.

We practiced every afternoon for two and a half hours. Shirts off, hip-hop blasting on speakers—sun's out, guns out. The women's soccer team would walk by, the women's volleyball team. We'd hit the ball a little harder when they did.

We'd do crosscourt drills, volley-to-volley. We'd do side-to-sides, attack and defense, serve and return. Then, three times a week post-practice, we'd be up in the gym with the trainer. We did the same weight routine as the baseball team.

Why are you doing that, Luke repeated. You're gonna injure yourself, Luke said as we passed each other on our way to opposite sides of the court.

His shirt was off but mine was on.

I like to train, I said. Worry about yourself, I said.

It was a practice match, but the coach was perched on the

center-court steps in tinted Oakleys and a baseball cap like it was something official.

I bounced the ball three times, my standard routine, and I tossed the ball into the blue sky.

First serve—ace down the T. 15–love.

Let! Luke called. That was a let.

Then why didn't you play it? I said. We played lets in college.

I didn't know we were playing lets.

We always play lets.

I looked over at the coach—his lips were sealed, his face stone cold. He didn't give anything away. He didn't want me to beat Luke. He didn't want to give me more money.

We held serve all the way to 7–7. We were playing an 8-game pro-set. A super tiebreaker would have to decide it.

At 0–0 in the tiebreaker, Luke hit a big flat first serve with a little slice into the body, and I punted it back deep. We found ourselves locked into a crosscourt exchange, forehand to forehand, and then I sent a ball up the middle, to see what he would do, and he panicked. He didn't think I would be this close.

He sprayed the ball out, a floater.

I fist-pumped.

I looked at the coach.

Calm down, Luke said.

It's just practice, Martin said, one of the Frenchmen on the court next to us and Luke's housemate.

Pay attention to your own match, I said.

The coach said nothing.

At 8–7 with me serving, I hit an American kick out wide to his backhand, the ball jumping high after the bounce. I had him off the court, so I rushed the net. I didn't hug the line too tight as I split-stepped because I had the feeling he'd try to dip it crosscourt if he got to the ball, and he did, he did go crosscourt as he swatted at it, full extension, and I stabbed left with my backhand volley, the top part of my strings making contact with the ball in slow-motion, and I squeezed the handle just enough to keep the wrist stable, my feet underneath losing the grip of the court as I stretched for a dive like Boris Becker, the ball zooming straight ahead where it landed on the white line on the other side, unreachable, untouchable—a winner!

Out! Luke called as my hip met the cement of the court, my eyes on the line the whole time.

I got up just as quickly as I fell. I tossed my racquet.

Bullshit! That ball was in and you know it.

Non non, Jeremie said from sidelines, wagging a finger.

He's right, Martin his housemate said.

I looked at the coach.

It's his call, the coach said.

8–8. It should have been 9–7. I had another point to serve. I wanted to peg him. But I bounced the ball, I took a breath, I walked up to the line, and I went for the body slice. He hit it right into the net.

9–8, Luke serving.

One more point to go.

I could see the deep breaths heaving in his chest. He was nervous. I had him. First serve. He tossed the ball in front of him, a little low, and it went into the net.

Second serve. A high enough toss, but his body was a little slow to reach it, his arm was too tight, and he muscled a conservative spin serve, one that popped up nicely for my run around forehand, all the time in the world—BAM!

I sent it to the opposite corner and he barely got to it, sending up a nice ice-cream floater for me to pounce on, and I wound up my forehand as my feet danced around the ball lightly and just when I was about to take a big cut, I changed the trajectory of my stroke and went underneath the ball with a delicate downstroke cut—a dropshot barely gliding past the top of the net, trickling over. He scampered and sprinted, the soles of his feet making desperate little cries as he barely got to the ball, giving me a nice sitter. I was almost on top of the net and he was right there. I had the whole court, but we made eye contact and I sent the ball right into his abdominal crease. It made a loud thud, hitting him like an Amtrak, sending him back to the earth.

Final score: 10–8.

I had won.

I beat Luke, our #1 player.

We didn't shake hands.

I left him there.

I left them all there.

I walked past the coach, my body hot, steaming, in the twilight chill, and headed to the locker-room shower.

The next day courtside, Coach took me aside. His brown mustache bristled as he spoke.

You looked good out there yesterday. Proud of ya, kid, he said as he laid a hand on my shoulder.

Glad you thought so, I said.

I waited for it. I knew something was coming.

Your serve could use some more pop though.

Oh yeah?

Yeah. I want to see more mph on that thing. Come over here, he said, pointing to the back of the court where a rusted shopping cart of faded looking balls rested.

The winter sun was low, sending a shadow of the light pole across the net. It looked like a crucifix.

This is what you're going to do, he said. He was in nylon sweats. They sounded like tissue paper rubbing together as he walked.

He grabbed three balls and pocketed two. Then he stepped up to the service line, and without a racquet, he chucked the ball to the opposite fence. He hit it directly, high up. Then, he threw another, same thing—fence.

Now, he turned back to me.

I want you to throw the ball as hard as you can.

How many? I asked.

The whole basket.

We're going to do this every day, he said. He left me there, and I grabbed a handful of balls. They were dead, shorn of hair, and with a gentle squeeze I could make the rubber meet.

Oh, he said, as he was walking away. Our next match is in two weeks. We have a bye-week this week. I'm going to give you a shot at the 3-line. Singles, he said.

I threw a ball—fence.

Another—fence.

Good, coach said. Very good, he said again, his voice echoing down the concrete pavilion just beyond the courts.

I threw my heart out.

I did this every day for two weeks.

The day of the match, I got to the van early. It was an away game, and I sat in the back with my headphones on. I had oatmeal that morning. A banana. I drank some water with electrolytes. My teammates—they ate donuts, hungover, still stoned.

When we got to the courts, I did my usual routine. Some jump rope, a stretch, some band work. My shoulder felt a little tighter than usual. A little sore. I tried to rub it out.

My teammates, they didn't say good luck. I went to the match court alone.

My opponent was decked out in a blue polo and orange shorts—his school colors. He was from Germany. Tall. Big, heavy serve. I could see it in the warm-up.

I took a few volleys and pointed my finger up to the sky—the universal sign for overheads. He fed me a lob, a little short, and I volleyed it back softly, and he fed me another, this one just right, and I swung a little too hard, a little fast, and that's when I felt it—a pop. I put my hand up, told him to stop, and I rotated my shoulder in its socket backward, then forward, backward, then forward, and when I raised my arm up to test it, I felt a pinch.

I took another lob, and when I tried to meet the ball with my racquet, there was no weight behind it, no muscle. Spaghetti. Then, I felt a crazy shooting pain.

I didn't make it past the warm-up.

My teammate Jeremie had to sub in.

I saw a specialist a week later—it didn't get any better—and scheduled an MRI for the following week. The results came back as a partial labrum tear. My options were surgery or physical therapy.

PT was a gamble. There was no telling when it would get better.

I was on the school insurance, so I opted for surgery.

Under the lights of the courts, I found my teammates wrapping up practice. They were grunting, joking, smacking balls at each other, then picking them up. Coach had them in a huddle—GO, COUGARS! they shouted, then dispersed.

They said hi to me.

They were kinder than before.

They were kinder because I no longer posed a threat.

The coach turned to me as I approached. He was clean shaven now, and his hazel eyes glinted a little. His jacket was zipped up all the way, the lights above us buzzing.

I'm out for the rest of the season, I said.

He shook his head understandingly.

I understand, he said. He laid a hand on my bad shoulder.

What he didn't know is what the orthopedic surgeon told me.

Thank you for letting me know, he said, as if to end the conversation. He was stepping away. He took another step back.

I wanted to talk to you about our deal, I said.

Deal?

There were moths above us, in a frenzy—their wings swatted the glass coverings of the lights. They were trying to get in.

You said if I break the top three, I'd get 75 percent next year.

That's right.

I broke the top three.

The coach, he sighed. I could see my breath ahead of me. I was in a T-shirt and shorts, my tennis shoes unlaced. It was 50 degrees out.

Now Ned, I gave you a shot at three, but you didn't play that match—remember?

That's because I got hurt.

And I am so sorry that you did. But I can't offer you that much money. We have another player coming from—

Remember the basket of balls? The throwing drill you had me do?

I stepped forward.

My doc said that most likely lead to the tear.

I've seen many injuries in my time, son. Tennis is not an easy sport on the shoulders.

The balls were too lightweight, I said.

Too light, I repeated, a little louder.

This is your fault.

Your fucking fault.

I stabbed my finger into the air. The coach, he blinked a little.

I suggest you go home now and get some rest. We can talk more tomorrow.

My finger was still pointed at him as he walked away.

The doctor said had I thrown another basket like that, I may have had nothing holding my shoulder together.

On the last day of the semester, I didn't wake up until 11. I was up all night. I wasn't studying. I bought half an ounce of cocaine at a house party from the guy who lived below me. We made the exchange at the side of the house next to the hose, the bathroom window. I could hear a dude peeing in the toilet.

I paid double for it. I didn't care. I didn't go to class. I didn't take my final.

In my dorm on the laminate coffee table was a ground beef taco left from the night before. I took a bite. The meat was cold, the hard shell starting to stale. I set up another line on my desk. I put my head down and then lifted it up.

In the bathroom, I looked in the mirror and breathed fast.

I smacked the glass with the flat of my palm and broke something in the medicine cabinet.

When I arrived at coach's office, he was there. I didn't even knock. I walked down the hall and grabbed the handle of his office door with the half window, and threw it open. The nailhead-trimmed chairs were made of real leather. Someone was sitting across from him, an administrator. I got behind the desk so fast that the colleague in suit-and-tie didn't even have a chance to stand.

I was on top of the coach, my knees on his thighs, the chair tipping over until we slammed back to the the carpet. I had him pinned down. My right hand began to throb. It was bleeding, my knuckles. I broke his nose, his face. They were pulling me away. He was screaming into his hands, but I didn't hear him. It took two people to lift me off of him. I kept throwing punches. Then, I punched the air. I was yelling. I didn't know what I was saying.

You ruined my fucking life.

You ruined my fucking life.

I quit tennis after that.

I returned to the house just as the mailman in the mail truck pulled away from the curb and drove away.

I saw a stack of letters in our mailbox—the lid wasn't flush. I fingered through them like vinyl at a record store when I paused on one and plucked it. *Wind & Sea* was printed on the lefthand side. Was this the first? How many of these had come? Had my wife intercepted one?

I folded it in half and put it in my pocket.

The racquetball court was dark inside except for some lit candles on the ground. There were two rectangular pillows about six feet apart, and my coach Joachim was seated crossed-legged on one of them, the candles in between. I gave the open door a knock.

Take a seat, Joachim said without opening his eyes.

As he spoke, the flames were slightly disturbed.

What are we doing?

We are working on your mental game.

I let my racquet bag slip off my shoulder, and I unlaced my tennis shoes but kept my socks on. I sat down on the pillow, really a cushion from a couch, and I tried to cross my legs. My hips were tight, my knees wanting to rise, so I pushed them down with my elbows. I felt a stretch. I looked up to face Joachim.

Are your eyes closed?

I closed them.

Yes.

Now follow my lead, he said. Think about a person you love. What do you feel inside? Maybe it's warmth? Allow it to be felt, whatever the feeling.

I thought of my son.

Joachim chanted some words. He told me to let this person go.

The scent of the candles smelled like lavender. They smelled good.

Now, he began, I want you to think of a person who has caused great difficulty in your life. It could be someone from long ago, or it could be someone now, Joachim continued. What do you feel? Has the warmth inside your body disappeared? Bring awareness to these feelings and just let them be.

Think of an angry moment with this person, Joachim said. Let the moment go. Let the person go.

He moved on. I heard the word "community." I opened my eyes and watched Joachim's lips move. I watched the smoke rise between us. The air was thicker now. I had trouble breathing. I coughed.

Okay, Joachim said, his eyes popping open. That's it for today!

He leaned forward and blew out the candles, then stood up.

How do you feel? he said.

Good, I said.

Yeah?

I do, I said.

He crossed the room and turned on the lights. The LEDs above flickered on. The ceiling must have been twenty feet high.

I gathered myself up. I put on my shoes, shouldered my bag. I was about to leave.

Oh, and don't forget the check, Joachim said.

He registered my surprise.

You can leave it with the front desk later today or tomorrow, he said.

I pushed open the glass door from the racquetball facility and met the bright light outside. I could feel it in my neck, the tightness. There must have been a knot in there.

Let the person go, Joachim had said.

My stepfather.

I felt something scraping my arm as I walked. My bag wasn't zipped up all the way, and the rough headguard of my racquet was poking out and rubbing against me.

I pushed it in and zipped the bag up, so that nothing was showing from inside.

I bought an indoor Ring camera on Amazon and then archived the purchase so it was hidden from my wife. Then, when it arrived, I mounted it on the wall directly above an electrical socket in my son's room.

The night the camera was installed, I made sure it was on, that my phone was connected to it, that I could speak into it.

Testing, testing, I said, while my son was in the shower.

Dad! I need a towel.

I rushed over to the bathroom, wiped his eyes.

In his bedroom, I watched him change slowly, clumsily into his PJs. Then, I showed him the purple gummy that was supposed to be a bee. It looked more like an alien with tentacles.

What's that, Dad?

This will help you sleep better, I said. They're called Zarbee's. I gave it to him and he licked the coated sugar suspiciously as I sat on his bed near the edge.

Good, right?

He put it in his mouth and chewed. When he was done, I gave him a sip of water from his water cup. I kept his night light on. I said good night, and he pulled the blankets over his head.

Downstairs, I waited five minutes on the couch until he was out. Then, I grabbed my tennis bag, the basket of balls, my keys. I opened the front door slowly, quietly, without a creak.

I drove to the club to hit some serves.

They say if you practice at night, the ball is exponentially bigger the next day when you play.

This holds true because I absolutely crushed my ladder match the following morning.

And when I came home that night, I opened my son's door to find him in a deep, deep sleep.

I petted his head.

Good boy, I said. Good boy.

* * *

The next night, after tucking my son in, I found myself at the club bar. When I finished my third Dark and Stormy, I noticed the motion alert notification on my phone. Next to me at the bar was Burris.

Fuck, I said.

The bar was loud.

I put the phone up to my ear, plugged my other ear with a finger.

Dad! I need to pee, Dad!

My son, he sounded groggy from the Zarbee's.

Everything okay? Burris said in his apres-ski windbreaker.

My son needs to pee.

Where is he?

He's home in bed.

Well, isn't your wife home?

I gotta jam, I said.

My son was screaming now. He said he couldn't hold it.

I ran down the club stairs as I tried to speak to my son via the Ring microphone, and on the last step I tripped.

Oh my god, are you okay? It was the front-desk girl.

I was flat on my stomach on the hardwood floor, and my phone was still in my hand, face down.

When I stood up, my screen was cracked, and I had a cut right in between my wrist creases.

I drove through two red lights, the touchscreen of my phone no longer working. My right wrist was bleeding. I found an old wet wipe now dry, stiff, and yellowed between my seat and the center console. I pressed into it hard as I steered with my bad hand.

I pulled into the driveway, and the moment I opened the front door, I yelled to my son, Daddy's here!

I bolted up the stairs two at a time, but then I saw the light, the light from his room falling into the dark hallway. The door was open, and I could see inside his lit room. My wife was holding him, sitting with him on the bed. His eyes were wet, and he looked at me. Then, she looked at me too, over her shoulder. She gave me a stare that aged me five years right then and there.

She ran the bath, changed him as I watched from his bathroom doorway. I made myself useful. I grabbed his wet PJs, his soiled bedsheets, and I put them in the washer immediately.

Then, I snuck into our master bath, and swished around some Listerine. I used some eye drops.

I took a deep breath and I waited for her in the bedroom.

I heard her emerge from our son's room a few minutes later. She shut his door carefully, quietly. I stood up from where I was sitting on the edge of our bed.

She entered ours.

Where the fuck were you? she said. She was still in her black travel blazer, her long black skirt, her purple turtleneck. Her hair was up, and the gold hoop earrings were still in her ears.

There was an emergency.

What kind of fucking emergency?

Our neighbor down the street lost his dog.

I felt the sweat trickle down my arms.

You left our son home alone in the middle of the night because of a fucking lost dog?

It was an emergency.

I don't give a shit. It isn't your problem!

I took a deep breath, reached out to touch the air between us gently.

Which neighbor?

Two houses down. You don't know him.

When did you become friends with this neighbor?

A year ago.

I've never heard you talk about him. What's his name?

Jerry.

Jerry?

Jerry. His wife just left him. He needed a hand, and Freddie was sleeping. I didn't know what to do, I panicked. He called me crying. The dog, it's all he has, you know? This beautiful Labrador with a coat so nice it looks like chocolate.

I've never seen a chocolate Lab on our block before.

That's because you're always working.

What's the dog's name?

Fido.

And you needed your car because?

Jerry had been hitting the bottle. I drove in case we needed wheels.

My wife, she just stared at me.

I don't care if he was on his deathbed and needed your help. You don't leave our son home alone, ever.

Understood, I said.

Don't ever do that again.

I won't, I said.

Your wrist is bleeding. Don't get it on the carpet.

She flicked the lights on in her walk-in closet and disappeared. I heard drawers being opened and shut as she changed.

The next morning, I was up before dawn.

Downstairs, I regarded the cannister of coffee beans, a bottle of bourbon—my life choices.

I uncorked the bottle and poured myself a thumb.

Then, I ground the beans in the burr grinder, trying to erase everything from the night before with the sound.

Sunday was Match Day, and Frederick came with. He was part of the process now. No complaints were made, and we doctored up a simple excuse for his mother—an educational excursion!

Fun, she said, with her hair tied in a low pony, but I could tell she didn't mean it. I didn't care though. Eyes on the prize.

The night before, I made a quick run to the club, where I purloined a micro-shear from the pro shop. In the car ride, I handed the blue-handled cutters to my son.

Now here's what you're going to do. Our opponents will set their bags down before we play the match. I want you to go to each bag like a silent ninja, unzip them, and find their racquets. Then you'll stick your hand in with those shears and cut their strings.

In the rearview, I clocked his bright oval eyes.

Yes, Dad, he said.

The park itself allowed for Maddock to recruit any player in the area he wanted. With *Wind & Sea*, I was under contract to only recruit members from the club. Maddock could roster Pete Sampras if he wanted to.

The park had a baseball field, a playground, some basketball courts. There were no special features to this park. It was a park. With the plan in place, I warmed up with my guys, my son waiting intently by the sidelines. Stout was still out.

Minutes before the match, I alerted Maddock of the change, that instead of defaulting a singles line, I would now need to play singles and default a doubles line.

You know you're not supposed to do that, Maddock said. A last-minute change like that.

If it's too much of a problem, I suppose you could just admit defeat right now then?

How about I just make note of this, buddy?

Frederick was crouched near a fountain where some of the player bags rested and Maddock's guys, unaware of their belongings, loafed around.

Are you playing today? I said, keeping it going.

I am not, he said. Why?

Because, let me know when you do play. I'd love to kick your ass.

Out of the corner of my eye I saw my son stand straight and pace back to a bench. He gave me the thumbs-up, and I rallied my men, Burris and Snider, for a quick huddle.

We made our way to our respective courts, where I met my opponent, a player I hadn't seen before. His name was Todd Pinderhaas.

We were about to spin for side and serve when Burris yelled.

Fuck!

I turned my head to see why.

Burris was holding two of his racquets in the air, and right smack in the center of both, there was a gap in the strings.

What the fuck! Snider said, not far from him, holding up his only racquet, and that's when Frederick, my son, started to cry. He had cut the wrong strings.

I assure you, we don't need to cheat to beat you guys, Maddock said a few minutes later. So no, we did not tamper with your equipment.

My son was beside me, sullen, but not crying, looking down.

Do you still want to play your singles line, Ned? Maddock queried.

I looked at him square in the face.

I came here to play, I said.

Todd's our 4.5 ringer. Don't let his rating deceive you, Maddock said, giving me a wink.

I gave my son my phone to occupy himself. He sat at the table with an umbrella hole but no umbrella.

I knew I was in trouble in the warm-up. Pinderhaas was my worst nightmare—a scrappy, off-pace moonballer. My fears were confirmed when the match started. Our first point, his service game, was a long backcourt exchange. I moved him side to side, front and back, and he returned everything high and deep, no pace. He was speedy—light on his feet. What this meant was I had to work extra hard to generate power. Mid-rally, eight shots in, I felt winded. I grew impatient. I went for a low percentage winner up the line, and I sprayed it just wide. Then, he was ready to serve the next point, already bouncing the ball, but I was still catching my breath. I was on his time though.

Ten minutes later, I found myself down 3–0, and five minutes later it was 5–0, Pinderhaas to serve. The first point of the game, Pinderhaas tossed the ball up in the air, then caught it. Then, he did it again—toss and catch. Even if he didn't like the toss, he could have apologized, and he didn't. It threw off my timing as a returner. That's why he was doing it. I looked at my son. My phone was in his lap, but his eyes were on me.

His serve came at me, and I shanked it. My rhythm was off. I slapped myself on the thigh with my free hand.

Pinderhaas was serving 15–love when he did it again, the toss-and-catch routine.

Point penalty! I called as he was bouncing, getting ready for another toss. He looked up at me, then off to the side at Maddock.

That was twenty-five seconds, I said. I counted. You only have 20 seconds between points to serve according to the league bylaws.

Woah woah woah, Maddock said. Are you an official?

Your player is disrupting play and delaying the game.

Answer my question, Maddock said. Are you an official?

Doesn't matter, he's breaking the rules.

Keep it quiet, or I will report you to the organization.

My dad's right! My son waved my phone in the air. I have a timer! I'm keeping track!

It's okay, Freddie, I said, smiling at him.

There was some excitement now, some fire.

And Pinderhaas was clearly rattled. He became self-conscious of his toss, his foot placement, his serve. He proceeded to double-fault the next three points in a row. I found myself with a break-point opportunity, and I was able to capitalize with a put-away volley.

Let's goooo! My son cheered.

I was able to bring it all the way back to 5–4. I had a chance.

But my body, it didn't hold. My legs, they started to give out. The first point of the game was a minimum twenty-ball rally, and I went down with an unforced error into the net. Pinderhaas had me where he wanted. He chopped me up, and I lost the game and the set.

My son looked up at me from the phone and made me a heart sign with his hands. He looked sad for me. I loved the little guy.

I didn't have any fight in me after that. I lost the next set without winning a game. I wanted to get off the court as fast as possible.

We shook hands at the net after the match.

That first set was a battle, Maddock said to me wistfully.

May do you some good to look at the rulebook sometime, I said.

Are you giving me homework? Maddock said.

Let's go, son, I said to my boy.

Freddie put his hand in mine.

Come on, Dad, my son said. It's okay.

Dear Loraine,

Our son took the loss the hardest. He cried the whole way home, and thankfully when we returned, you were off somewhere, so I calmed him down with popsicles, a run to the comic-book store, and television. Yes, I did reprimand him. I know you may say that he shouldn't have been involved in the first place, but he wanted to be involved. And I'm not trying to place blame here, but we truly lost before the matches even started today. As captain, I felt responsible, and I lost my focus early on. I had one loaner for Burris, and Snider had to play with his wife's over-sized racquet that was somewhere in the trunk of his car. It was a bad loss.

The fact is, we need Roland.

What happened? said Mason the personal trainer.

So tell me about the match, queried Ken.

I can't believe it, said the voice in the steam room.

The hall of photos in the men's locker room was gap-toothed—mine was missing. Someone had removed it.

Carlin, she walked right by me. She wouldn't even look at me.

Ned, how did you let this happen, the front-desk girl said over the PA system.

The teenager running the snack shop threw a brown banana at me, and then, despite myself, and with some self-disgust—I was hungry—I ate the soggy banana.

I heard you lost, said the bagger at the grocery store.

The ATM wouldn't accept my card, and when the bank-teller woman saw me approach, she went on lunch.

I ordered a coffee and put sugar and half and half in it, and in the car, Charlie Puth's "Loser" played on the radio.

Oh, I'm such a loser.

I sang along.

No you're not, Dad, my son said.

I think we should take a break, Joachim said.

I agree, I said.

It's what's best.

Okay, I said. Sure.

It doesn't mean we can't try again later. You got game, kid, but—

But . . . ?

I think you gotta work on what's between the ears if you know what I'm saying.

I took that to heart.

See you around, he said, and before I could say anything, he had already hung up.

I looked for him in the nearby rundown port town under the bridge. The bridge was green steel. It looked like a low serpent with a slightly arched back. The water below was dark like oil. People flung themselves from this bridge.

I parked underneath it and could see across the bay to the downtown.

I walked along. There was a pallet of wood and some discarded 32-ounce brown glass bottles of Corona. There was a cracked leather La-Z-Boy with a Mickey Mouse doll resting on the seat cushion, head flung back. There was an upturned shopping cart.

The island express boats were docked here. The half-day boat was also here, and nearby was a boatyard.

People were lining up for the express, and a building, a small little ferry station, stood nearby. I walked to it, grabbed the door handle, walked inside. Varnished wood benches, vending machines, a coffee stand. There was a ticket booth with a wraparound line of families, old couples, the occasional singleton. I fingered the photo in my pocket. I'd have to wait awhile to speak to the ticket seller.

Back outside, I followed the blue signs with arrows for the boatyard entrance. The area was fenced off from the rest, and once I found the opening, I saw the towering blue handling crane with a yacht suspended in the air. There was a yard laborer there with a paintbrush painting the hull red. He had on yellow deck boots, gray jeans, a soiled looking T-shirt. His face had been tanned a hundred thousand times.

Excuse me, I said, the photograph already in my hand.

He looked at me, his lips slightly parted—he was in the zone, high off the fumes, and I was distracting him from the work at hand. I could smell the paint, the scent of dead fish, of rot, of salt.

I'm looking for someone, I said. I showed him the photograph. He squinted a little, put the paintbrush down, the tin of red paint, on the gravel, the dirt, beneath him. He took the photograph from my hands.

This your friend?

I nodded.

He gave me back the photograph.

He's been missing, I said.

He bent down with a groan, grabbed the brush, the paint, resumed his strokes.

Well, he's been around here. Causin' some trouble. They chased him out of here a few days ago.

What kind of trouble?

He broke into my friend's 'sixty-six Chris-Craft a week ago down at the yacht club. The ole slippin'-into-the-boat slip. Was found in there taking up residence. Stole a little VHF radio and a portable heater, too. Not sure what the radio will do for him.

Where'd he run off to?

By the time the cops came, he was long gone. He can't be far though. They're all around here.

Could I give you my number? In case you see him again?

The man looked at me like he didn't hear me.

Thanks for your time, I said.

From the car, I called Vernon and told him the news.

Roland is going to do what Roland is going to do, he said. He was here last night in fact, he said.

What do you mean?

I had fallen asleep as per usual in the living room when I heard a loud repeated BOOM! I thought I was dreaming it. Then, I woke up to shards of glass flying at my fuckin' face from my broken window and a tennis ball nearly knocking the TV set over. I look out and who do I see? My son Roland. Roland was out there on the street tossing and serving, aiming for the house. The neighbors' lights were on, families gathered, standing in their doorways, on their balconies, dogs barking. And he just carried on like he was on the court, bombing first serves at my home. When he ran out of balls, he packed up his racquet in his bag and threw it all on the front lawn. And you know what he was trying to tell me with that gesture, throwing his bag on my front lawn?

What?

That he was done. Done with tennis. And you know what? I'm done with him.

What about his racquets?

Well they're on my front lawn if you want them.

An hour later I swung by Vernon's. I saw the broken window, the tennis balls scattered around the front yard. I grabbed his red Wilson bag and put it in my trunk.

Don't put me with Snider anymore, Burris said.

Why not?

He played like a fuckin' asshole.

Snider is a nice guy, I said. He's a good doctor.

He's an asshole. He plays like an asshole.

I don't get it, I said.

He's an asshole doctor, Burris said.

No he's not, I said. He's a foot doctor.

I found a lone backcourt at the club to practice serves. The low sun had disappeared behind a sheet of marine layer, and I set up a couple of cones, the ones with holes in them so they wouldn't tip over in the breeze. I heard laughter, a woman's voice, and right from the start, I belted the ball as hard as I could, and my shoulder let me know that that was a mistake. I kept going. I shanked the fifth or sixth one, a new ball still with nice fuzz to it, and I followed its path as it soared in the sky like a foul ball.

My search led me closer to the pleasured voices. I bisected a nearby court and unlatched the gate to the garden alley with circular pavers. I could hear a man now. I shifted some bushes with the head of my racquet. Then, they saw me and I saw them. The court was missing a windscreen. All that separated us was a fence. Thiago had his shirt off, and his chest hair looked groomed, dry, and soft, and Carlin had her hand pressed against him. Thiago's white shorts were almost see-through, and Carlin's top had a deep plunge in the neckline and her skirt was pleated. Balls were scattered around them. I turned away.

Hey there, Ned, Thiago said. This is Carlin.

We know each other, I said.

Hi, Ned, Carlin said to me, letting her hand fall.

Don't mind me, I'm just looking for a ball.

You can have some of ours if you want, Thiago said. My student here is a little unfocused.

That's because you're a lousy coach, Carlin said, poking him.

Hey, I heard about the match, Ned.

They need you, Carlin said to Thiago.

Oh, we'll manage just fine. Well, enjoy your lesson, I said to Carlin, and that was that.

I never did find that ball.

After three months, my wife started pumping and I started feeding. Before that, I took up residence in the home office. I had a futon in there—that is where I slept.

In the middle of the night, if one of my earplugs fell out, I'd hear his hungry cries. I'd stay put. I'd roll another earplug into my ear until all I could hear was the beating of my own heart.

My wife and son were attached all times of day—in bed together, on the couch. He was either sucking on one of her breasts, or nuzzled against her chest. I'd watch them sleep together in broad daylight, both mouths agape. I paid for a night nurse. I masturbated. I was working fourteen-hour days. That was my contribution.

But three months in, my wife reached her breaking point. Her skin grew paler, the rings under her eyes darker.

Soon my wife stopped pumping, and we switched to formula. I did the mixing. I put him to bed. My wife—she went back to work. The daycare was almost as much as our mortgage.

I'd sit in the rocking chair with the bottle's nipple in my son's mouth, his big eyes watching me as he sucked. Slowly they'd start to dim and close. I was the one that fed him. I became mother bird.

He became mine, too.

She's married, you know, I said to Thiago.

Oh I know, Thiago said. I'm a big boy.

Carlin was next to him, her back to his, socializing with another member. They were already familiar, locked in, like a couple, an occasional affectionate touch on the shoulder, the lower back, as they spoke to their respective party.

I watched the bartender make my cupid cocktail, the crack and drop of the fresh egg, the double shot of sherry, a sprinkle of cayenne, shaken well, strained into a glass goblet. It was placed before me, and I left it there, staring down at its foamy top.

It will only go so far, I said.

I'm not thinking about the future, Thiago said. I like to live in the present, he declared as he raised his dirty martini to his stubbled face. He was in a waffled buttonless polo, burnt orange. It looked like something she had picked out for him, something she bought for him while they shopped together at the mall like teenagers.

Clearly, I said.

What?

You said you're not thinking about the future, and that is evident.

Sounds like you know from experience.

Not with her.

Oh, I know that. Buddy, he said, while laying a heavy hand on my shoulder and leaving it there. You okay? You haven't touched your drink yet. Drink up. Be merry!

Why? I said. It's not Christmas.

Every day is Christmas. Every day is a gift!

You've been drinking too much.

I grabbed my drink. I took a sip.

Let's get out on the court soon, he said.

Let's play a ladder match. Make it official, I said.

Love that idea!

Before I could say anything else, he was turning, talking to someone else, so I pushed off. I saw Bray down the bar, a little stumbly, with a pint of something dark, eyes glazed, looking everywhere and nowhere all at once. I didn't want to talk to him.

Carlin, in a tight blue denim romper was alone now, so I cut in close.

I spoke to your beau, I said. Congratulations.

You sound bitter, she said. I looked at the drink before her, sweating. It was also a dirty martini.

You know I beat him the last time we played. Straight sets.

I'm not surprised, Ned. You're a great player. Everyone here knows that.

And you're married.

We've already been over this.

Don't drag him into it.

Would it be any different if it was with you?

Why him?

Why not? He made a move first.

He's a baseliner. He never makes the first move.

Well, how come you didn't then?

I finished the rest of my drink. I was about to respond when a hand gripped my shoulder. I felt the nails. It was Bray, in my face. I could smell the chocolate stout on his breath.

Hey, we need to talk, he said, pulling me away, and pushing me down into the brown leather loveseat. He plopped down next to me.

You need to put me in singles the next match. I'm sick of this doubles crap.

He started listing guys on our team, their stats. This season, past seasons. Then he talked about the players on opposing teams, and how they did in the league, in tournaments, and how there was six degrees of separation between all of us, meaning he had already inadvertently beaten Federer, Nadal, Djokovic, all of the greats in fact, dead greats too, and I nodded and nodded. I thought of my own game, the team, where I would be if I hadn't quit playing, how Thiago wasn't even that good. I didn't understand why he was #1 on the ladder ahead of me—I needed to speak to Ken about this. I was better than him. And Roland. Roland was the best of us all. Roland in his prime would have wiped these guys off the map. Roland had a genuine chance against Federer, Nadal, Djokovic. Maybe not now, but maybe now. Time was running out. The season was almost over. We needed him for our match against Maddock's team. I needed more time. My wife, I needed her to stay put with our son. My son, he didn't like tennis. What a disappointment. It was all such a disappointment.

My son—where was he now?

The next morning, before I went to the port, I took my son to the club. As we pulled into the lot, a line of cars were ahead of us, children exiting minivans in droves. Many of the children were in oversized camp T-shirts, bathing suits and trunks visible here and there. They wore backpacks and carried sack lunches.

What's this, I said.

When we entered the club, I popped into Ken's office.

Summer sports camp, he said, drinking a cup of tea, the teabag drifting and bumping his upper lip when he took a sip. He scooched a paper flyer forward, an 8.5 × 11 sheet of blue. Baseball, basketball, swimming, arts and crafts, lunch included.

I want to do a sports camp, Frederick said.

Well, Ken said, consulting his computer monitor. It just so happens that one family had to pull out last minute. I just need you to sign this waiver, Dad, and Frederick is all set.

Charge it to my card?

We'll charge it to the credit card we have on file.

I signed the waiver. Then, I drove home and grabbed a pair of swim trunks, some goggles, a change of clothes, and stuffed it in Frederick's school backpack. Back at the club, I handed the counselor a tube of sunscreen. Pickup wasn't until 3 P.M. I had five hours.

I looked for Roland. I parked underneath the shadow of the bridge. Atop a rock from the break wall, there was a pile of uncooked asparagus.

Right next to a low, squat brick building, an abandoned warehouse, I found a floral blanket neatly spread. On this blanket was a plastic bottle of maple syrup, half full. There was also a small little tent with a loose leash nearby. The owner and animal were nowhere in sight.

Then I heard a noise. It sounded like someone coughing, but it was just a skateboard going over cracks in the sidewalk.

In a parking structure overlooking the water, I could hear the echo of a mother singing "Twinkle Twinkle Little Star." A man screamed HA from the driver side of his parked car.

His car had no wheels. It rested on cinderblocks.

I watched a man beat his forehead against a curb. Not far from him was a squashed banana. It looked like a dead bird with the legs over here, the wings over there.

I met a man named Ray. He wore leather boots with the American Flag on them over his torn jeans. He spoke of Santa Rosa and San Bernardino. His wife, he said, has been in the hospital since February. He pointed out to the ocean.

There are UFOs out there deep in the water, he said.

I showed him the picture of Roland. He said he'd keep an eye out for me. He told me about his van, how he turned it into a mini camper. I gave him my number. I trusted him.

We were supposed to be training. It was a Sunday, so there was no academy that day. We were on one of the backcourts, the one with the abandoned field behind it. The field was full of weeds with bald patches of dirt. There were goal posts still there, the netting gone. All that stood was the metal skeletons.

We found a shopping cart full of old balls—once yellow, now white and shorn of hair with very little air—within the unlatched wooden shed on the side of the court. These balls were our ammo, and we hit them as hard as we could straight into the sky like rockets, deep into the neighboring field.

Let's see who can hit it the farthest, Roland said.

He had an advantage. He was older and stronger. All his balls landed near the farthest goal. They'd stop just short.

When it was my turn, I could only make it halfway down the field.

Try again. Think of something that pisses you off. Like this! he said, loading up his legs, then tossing the ball forward, running toward it with an open-faced racquet, and *boom*, blasting it to the moon.

My turn. I thought of something. Someone. I hit the ball as high and as hard as I could, and like a golfer I watched the trajectory, the arc, and descent. It landed closer to Roland's.

Roland launched another into the sky. I did the same.

We went like this for a while.

It felt good.

We hit every single one. When we were done, we pushed the empty cart back into the shed. We sat on the bench slumped and tired, side-by-side.

My old man fuckin pisses me off so much, Roland said.

Same, I said, the field now salted with the white, dead balls.

I needed a hot shower, a fresh shave. I'd do that after, I told myself.

I needed to steam first.

When I approached the glass door, it was dark inside, the air thick and opaque. Some of the steam sucked out as I pulled the handle and opened. I saw a spot on the bench to sit on as my eyes adjusted. I pulled the towel from my waist and folded it into a square before taking a seat.

I hear the team is doing well, said the voice.

We're tied for first.

Stay the course.

Trying, I said. Hard to juggle everything.

Juggle what?

My guilt.

Guilt?

I should be looking for a job.

Right now, tennis is your job. You're the captain of the team.

I'm also a father.

You're doing fine.

I could be spending more quality time with him.

He's so young. He isn't going to remember this. But you will. You will remember this season for the rest of your life. This is your big comeback, remember?

I nodded. I was enveloped in a dark hot cloud.

Sacrifices need to be made, Ned. This is about you right now.

Right, I said.

You're a champion in the making.

When I stepped on the court, no one greeted me. They were all there, warming up. Thiago was even there. I had not invited him. Joachim was stationed at the farthest net post next to his cart of balls on wheels. Even though I had commissioned him for this live ball session, he turned away as I approached. He was there to feed balls, to keep score during the games.

I was doing this for the team. I had organized it. The morale was down, and we needed a boost.

I set my bag down, grabbed my jump rope, jumped. I did a couple toe touches before grabbing my racquet.

I stood near the alley looking at my players scattered around the court, heads down, like children who had recently been scolded.

Can someone warm me up?

Stout stepped forward and stood across the net from me. I stroked a few strokes, jabbed a couple volleys, pointed up for a lob.

I wasn't quite ready.

During one-up, two-back, Burris hit a swinging volley right at me—I turned right in time so it hit me in the scapula instead of the throat. He didn't even apologize.

The next game of one-up, one-back, Stout nailed an approach shot right into my shin.

Then, during 101, Bray got me right in the ribs.

To make matters worse, Joachim called the score wrong. It was supposed to be 57–54, but Joachim reversed it, giving the other side a 3-point lead.

That's not the score, I said to Joachim.

Yes, it is, Joachim said.

No it isn't. I told him the real score.

Why don't you focus on playing. Might serve you better.

Why don't you learn how to fucking count.

Calm down, Thiago said.

You're supposed to be on my side. We're on the same team.

Just settle down, buddy. You're running a little hot today, Thiago said.

The next point, the other team sent up a high lob, and Thiago, at net, let it go, making no attempt for it at all. It was all on me at the baseline. I watched Thiago's little floating head out of the periphery of my vision, and I let the ball take a high bounce. Then, I struck the overhead as hard as I could, right into the back of Thiago's skull. It made a dull thud on contact. Thiago dropped to his knees, then curled forward. He was nursing the back of his head with both hands interlaced.

Everyone ran over, even Joachim. They circled around him. I stood my ground.

You're a fucking asshole! Stout said.

Completely unhinged! Burris said.

Snider with squinty eyes wagged his head at me. He looked deeply disappointed.

This? This is how you treat me as captain? I began. It's become a full-time job, dealing with the lot of you. I feel like I'm babysitting a bunch of babies! This is the appreciation you show me?

Someone get him some ice, Snider, the foot doctor said, and Burris ran off the court, presumably to the ice machine.

Fuck you, I said. Fuck you all.

I packed my things, grabbed my canteen, hoisted my bag.

When I looked back at Thiago, he was seated on the court. His eyes met mine. They were wide, maybe a little wet—the eyes of sad, sick seal stuck on land.

I left the court.

I didn't pay Joachim either.

After dinner, I remained at the dining table, sitting across from my wife. My plate was still there with some pushed-aside yams and the remaining silver flakes of a baked salmon. My wife drank from a wide-hipped wine glass, a Claret, despite the fish. Covered up in a shirt jacket with a T-shirt underneath, she looked at me directly over the edge of her glass as she took a sip. Our son was in the other room playing with the TV on. All I had was a glass of water in front of me, but suddenly I felt the urge for something hard, straight, brandy, whiskey.

My wife began, So how's the job hunt going?

It's going.

Any bites?

Nope.

No leads?

No leads.

Have you spoken to a recruiter?

It's on my to-do list.

Oh. I didn't know you kept one.

When I got up from the table, the chair underneath me screeched, and one of the wooden legs felt wobbly. I could tell that at any moment it would give.

I went to the bar and pulled a glass from the cabinet. Then, I poured myself some Old Rip Van Winkle. I took a couple gulps while standing there. I poured myself a little more before returning to the table.

I set the glass down on the table—a little splashed—but the chair, it didn't give when I sat down heavily.

I keep it all in here, I said, knocking my temple hard with a finger.

My wife took another sip, a breath, closed her eyes, opened them, regarded me.

I'm sorry, she said. I know that came across the wrong way.

You mean you didn't say it right.

Yes, you're right. Let me rephrase—do you need me to help you?

What makes you think I need help?

Honey, my wife said, placing a flat hand on the table. Her fingernails were naked, a little long. All of the sudden, she looked very tired to me.

She said, Honey, I've just been looking at our numbers. We have enough money to survive the summer, but come fall, I need your help again. She let that sit. I raised my glass, drank some more, and felt warm.

I need your help, she said.

Well, I am helping. I am taking care of our boy here. That's what you asked me to do, right?

You said you'd be looking for a job, Ned.

I am taking care of our son, and I am taking care of myself. I found tennis again, you know. I've reconnected with a part of me. I'm taking care of myself. Maybe you could do the same, I said, and my wife, she froze.

Excuse me, she said. I'm the one who is keeping a roof over our head. Maybe if I had a partner pulling his own weight, I could think about *taking care of myself.*

Maybe your priorities are off?

Wait, what? she said, almost knocking over her wine glass. Her head was turned slightly to the left now with the ridges of her forehead appearing, eyes narrowing.

I feel better than I've ever felt. When I'm on that court, I feel like myself again. And the scary thing is? I still have so much potential. I see those guys on the TV, playing professionally, and I'm right there. I know it. I can feel it. And you know what? If no one else knows that, that's okay. I don't need to be on the TV. But in my mind? I see myself and I'm happy. I feel like I'm going where I need to. I just need to keep going with this. I just need to keep going.

You just need to keep going.

Yes. I'm training every day. Improving every day. Things just take time, but I'm getting there.

Where exactly?

I'm close to reaching my full potential.

As a tennis player.

As me.

Okay, my wife said, pushing herself away from the table. She stood with her hands hovering in the air as if she might need to grab onto something. Okay, she said. Okay, she repeated, but she wasn't talking to me. She was talking to herself.

I sat at the table alone. I said what I needed to say. I sipped on the rest of my whiskey. There was no rush for anything anymore.

My wife had an old radio set from the thirties that her father passed down to her. It came from his father and his father before that—these were men of industry. It had a beautiful walnut finish and short stubby legs. It was about 10 inches in height. We kept it draped in the garage. We hadn't found a suitable place for it in the house yet. It was a little too wide for the mantel above the fireplace, and it distracted from the mounted flatscreen in the living room should we set it atop the console.

In a closed plastic bin next to it were some old dolls, also heirlooms from generations ago from the women in the family. They were metal-head dolls. They used to cry and sleep apparently. I selected the one with long mohair curls, about 20 inches in height. This doll could stand on its own—it had a staggered step.

I placed both of them in my large duffel bag below my racquets. They made for excellent targets on the court.

The metal-head doll lasted longer than the radio.

After I finished my last set of bench presses, a plate on each side, I cornered Mason, my trainer, in his office. His feet were propped up on the desk, clad in white-and-red high tops. He was holding a folded-back magazine, and on his head was a baseball cap, backward.

Sup, bud, he said, dropping the magazine into an open drawer, then closing it. His legs slinked back down to the ground.

You got a minute? I said.

Sure, what's up?

I looked over my shoulder and closed the door behind me.

I could see the blue vein of his bicep, his T-shirt sleeve barely concealing his deltoids.

I don't know how to say this, so I'm just going to say it.

He waited.

The suspense is killing me, he said.

Do you have any Arnolds?

Arnolds?

Yeah.

Like Arnold Palmers? What are we talking about here?

No like A-bombs.

He was wincing at me now.

Juice, I said. You know. I need some juice.

Roids?

Yeah.

You're joking.

I'm looking for an edge out there. I jerked my head to indicate outside of here. I'm no spring chicken, I said. I'm pushing forty, playing against guys half my age. I still have the game, and my mental faculties are sharp as a tack. But I need something to help get me across the finish line.

I pulled two bills from my pocket, cash back from my secret card that I obtained from the teller at the supermarket. I slid the cash onto the desk.

I'm going to pretend this conversation never happened.

Get me something good, I said.

I left the money on the desk.

The next morning, before dawn, I got a text.

Locker 32.

I drove to the club. It was 6 A.M. On my way to the locker room, I passed by the gym. There were only a few senior members in there, moving slowly from machine to machine. No sign of Mason.

When I got to locker 32, a day locker with no lock, I opened it and felt around. Then, I stood on my toes. On the little wooden shelf above the small double hook for clothes, there was nothing.

Maybe someone had got there before me, I thought.

Maybe someone had seen Mason slip something inside.

I called Mason right away. He picked up on the second ring.

Nothing's in here, I said. I'm here right now.

Look harder, he said.

I breathed in the sweaty musk. The locker needed to be aired out, wiped down, cleaned.

I am, I said.

Check the top.

I stood on my toes again.

No, the top, above the locker, his voice came louder, ringing in my ears.

Do you feel stronger yet? he asked. I heard an echo.

From what? I said. There's nothing in here.

From those calf raises you're doing to look inside.

The voice was coming from behind now, and I turned to see Mason standing there in jogging pants, a hoodie. His face was bright red, and he keeled over and cackled wildly.

You made my week, bud! he said.

He straightened up, reached in his pocket, tossed the two bills up in the air before he left.

I could hear him still laughing, hooting, down the hall.

My phone was still pressed to my ear.

I watched the money float down to the carpet.

My father was a good man, or so I was told, depending on who I asked. I never met him, so I can't really say what kind of man he was, a good man or a bad man or something in between.

My stepfather was not a good man.

I found street parking behind the gates of the country club. I nodded, waved at the red-vested valet, walked up the steps to the cherrywood double doors. I grabbed the bronze handle, stepped onto the white marble. There was a woman ahead of me in a puffer jacket, some tights, filling out a guest form.

And she can just walk right in, right? She can meet me on the court?

That is correct, the front-desk girl responded. We will just need to make a copy of her driver's license.

When it was my turn, I rattled off the four digits.

Ten twenty-three, I said.

The girl was in a turtleneck sweater, beige, and her nameplate was gold. She wore red lipstick, and her hair was down and brown, past her shoulders, parted down the middle. She regarded the computer in front of her, punched in the numbers. I studied the freckle on the ridge of her nose. Then with her blue eyes and a smile, she handed me two feathery, warm towels.

Welcome back, Mr. Lafferty.

Thank you, I said.

I went straight to the men's locker room and found a long vertical day locker to place my bag inside. The lockers were also cherrywood, and the carpet, it was a forest green, diamond patterned, the outline of the diamonds in gold. There was a man next to me, lacing his tan leather dress shoes. He stood up, grabbed his leather tote. Hello, I said as he approached.

He gave me a cautious-looking nod. As he rounded the corner and disappeared, I undressed. I kept my clothes and shoes in a pile underneath the bench. I turned on the jets of the jacuzzi. I freeballed it. I soaked myself.

Next was the steam room, the sauna.

Then, I took a scalding hot shower.

I threw the wet towels into a wooden hole and grabbed two more from a shelf above. I moussed my face with Kiehl's shaving cream, grabbed a blade. I squirted some mouthwash into a little cup, swished it around. I moisturized my face, my balls. I put some product in my hair. I looked at myself in the mirror. I looked perfectly normal. I looked well-adjusted. My eyes were a little red, but now that I was shaved, I looked like a man that had a late night at the office was all.

I stepped back into my tennis clothes. I grabbed my bag from the locker.

Before I made my way to the courts, I went up to the bar. It was 10:30 in the morning, but someone was there, polishing the bar with a brown rag. He was wearing red suspenders, a blue-striped dress shirt tucked into black slacks, a red tie.

You serving yet?

His hair was slicked back, black. The hand with the cleaning rag stopped, and the man regarded me.

What can I make you?

Old-fashioned, I said.

He brought out a block of ice and carved it with a small knife. He shaped the ice into a diamond. He dropped it into the glass.

Charge it to your account?

Please, I said. I gave him the last four digits, and I finished the drink in three big sips.

I ordered two more.

Center court was empty, recently resurfaced. All the courts were so. Dark green with white lines. Classic.

A man with white hair and an oversized racquet was hitting with the ball machine on a side court. I followed the back path under the canopy of a large oak. The trees were thoughtfully planned—they didn't hang over any of the courts, but just beside them, and the grass was well kept, trimmed. The birds chirped but not obnoxiously.

I couldn't spot any of their droppings anywhere. These birds with proper etiquette were sparse, hidden, happy, content.

Then I heard the deep shout—an assault to the almost silence. I heard the man's voice, not far, and then a ball being struck, smacking the privacy screen attached to the back fence. The windscreen was mesh—I could see through it, and I saw the man feeding balls, his back to me with a blue polo tucked into red shorts, a red cap. The man had wide shoulders, a stain of sweat down his spine. Across from him was a teenager, possibly his son, on the other side.

Where was that forehand yesterday, huh? When it counted?

The man fed another ball and the teenager belted it down the line, right to where I was standing behind the fence. I felt a puff of air as it struck, the clang of metal.

If you can't do this when it counts, you're never going to make it.

The young player, he kept belting. He had a beautiful game, world class.

As I rounded the perimeter, I watched him. He wore a yellow Nike Dri-FIT, and his blond hair peeked out the sides of his cap, giving his face a crown. He looked like a young prince.

You lose again, you're done, the man said.

Now pick them up, he said, as the junior approached the basket. The man grabbed an almost empty water pitcher, made his way to the far side to exit the court. I entered the gate closest to me.

That your pops? I asked the blond player.

He nodded.

I stepped on a ball, almost slipped. The son looked alarmed as I stumbled.

I'm okay, I reassured, finding my balance.

Hey! I yelled. Hey, pal! I yelled again. I stopped the father in his tracks. He looked at me threateningly over his shoulder, his instinct kicking in, and I continued.

Yeah you. Why don't you pick on someone your own size?

The son, he looked at me too.

Excuse me? the man said.

You heard me. Don't talk to your son that way.

Don't tell me how to talk to my son. Get off my court.

You get off, or I'll make you. Your job is done here. Take that pitcher and think about your actions. Go fill it up with water, water boy.

I grabbed a tennis ball and chucked it at the man, hard. It flew over his head like a missile. He ducked a little, but then faced me full frontal, like he was going to charge at me like a lineman.

I took off my shirt, threw it on the ground.

Bring it, fucker, I said, and the father, he did nothing. I looked at the father. I looked at the son. They were frozen there. I could feel the sun on my bare back.

Your son is very talented. Nurture that. Don't fuck it up! I said.

I picked up my shirt and walked off the court until I found the path again.

I journeyed on. I lifted my arms up and let the breeze circle around me, embrace me. It felt nice, this air. It smelled nice too. I was close to the pool now. I could hear splashes, little voices, the sound of the TV from the poolside café.

Up ahead, that's when I saw him coming. The man was in a blazer, steel blue. Khaki pants. Very official looking.

I walked toward him to meet him.

Can I help you? I said.

Could you put your shirt back on please.

I complied. It was inside out, my shirt, so it took some adjusting.

The man's light brown hair was thinning, but it was combed over to make it look full.

I'm Glen, the new GM here.

Nice to meet you, Glen.

I put my hand out for a shake, but he didn't shake it.

What was your name?

Rick, I said.

Rick. I think there's been a mistake if you wouldn't mind helping me.

A mistake?

It looks like Gina inputted the wrong member number.

Is that right?

She thought you were Mr. Lafferty, but Mr. Lafferty arrived ten minutes ago. What is your last name, Rick?

Bender.

The bartender didn't recognize you either, and Mr. Lafferty is a well-known patron. What are the last four numbers of your membership?

Ten twenty-two.

He removed his touch-screen phone from his pocket, typed with his thumbs.

A leaf fell from the tree above—I watched its slow descent.

Would you mind following me?

Sure thing, I said.

I followed Glen as we cut through the pool, walked alongside center court. It was now occupied with four women, all in skirts, playing doubles. We walked past the bar, the luxe gym.

Glen, would you give me a moment? I left my phone and wallet in my locker.

Glen turned to face me. He looked at me square in the face, the eye.

I'll be right back, I said. Promise.

Inside the locker room, I walked past the lockers, the sinks, the showers, all the way to the back. Members seated, standing, in the oblong-shaped jacuzzi—they all looked at me.

Then, I found it, the door.

Emergency

Exit Only

Door Must

Remain Closed

At All Times

I pushed it open with all my weight and saw the light.

The siren, it was going off now behind me as I ran.

I was back in the parking lot. There were cars, a detailer working on a cream-colored Porsche. I ran past the valet guy. He was on his walkie.

Hey! someone called behind me.

I got to my car. I unlocked it, threw my bag into the passenger seat, pressed the ignition button. In the rearview there was Glen as I drove away. He had his phone to his ear, and the girl was next to him, the valet guy too.

She was snapping photos of my car, my license plate.

In my humble opinion, the club wasn't worth the price you had to pay. Even if I had the money, I would never join.

Dear Loraine,

Today I diced an onion. It wasn't just any onion. It was a big yellow one almost the size of a watermelon. It must have been genetically enhanced. I had to use the meat cleaver, the one your uncle got us as a wedding gift from Japan. Damascus steel. And you know what's strange? I didn't tear up once. I sliced it into slices and then I chopped up those slices until all that was left was onion confetti. The whole operation took about five minutes, and I didn't cry, not once. My eyes, they were completely dry. I transferred my work from the cutting board into a salad bowl. Then, I went into the backyard and grabbed fistfuls and tossed it high into the sky. It felt a little like snow falling on me. It was really nice.

Dutifully,
Your Husband

Every week they ask you.
What's your rank?
How'd you do?
What round did you get to?
You lost to that guy?
Did you play consolation?
Why not?
Who won the tournament?
When's the next tournament?
How many double faults did you hit?
Did you serve and volley at all?
Did you hit any winners?
Any aces?
Any drop shots?
Any lobs?
Did you grind?
Did you give up?
Did you give 110 percent?
Did you skin your knees?
Did you roll an ankle?
Did they cheat?
Did you cheat?
Did you call a linesman?
Did you talk to your opponent?
Was his dad there?
Was the dad coaching?
Did you break his serve?
Did you break a racquet?
Did you bleed?
Did you hit him?
Every week they ask these questions, but they never ask one—

Did you have fun?
You are eleven years old.

When I entered the house, my wife was in the dining room with her laptop, a coffee mug, and opened mail scattered around her.

Be right down, I said as I snuck up the stairs before she could see me. I had just gotten off the court, my shirt still soaked. I changed into a pair of khaki shorts, a polo, and patted my wet head with a dry towel.

When I came back down, my wife's eyes were red, like she had been crying.

What's wrong, I said.

We're under water, she said. I don't know what do to, she said.

What do you mean?

One of our cards is maxed out and the second payment of our property tax is going to be due soon.

What about our savings?

There's nothing there.

Our checking?

She shook her head.

At one point there was discussion of me joining her father's business, the one her brother took over. They sold insurance for a living. I did not want to sell insurance. I wasn't a company man. I did not need any handouts.

I walked over to the pantry and poured some cashews into my cupped palm. I chewed on a couple, fisted the rest as I reasoned.

What about your father? I said.

What about you? she said.

Call your father, I said.

You call him, she said.

I'm not doing that.

I ate some more cashews. They were a little bland—could have used some salt.

My wife, she took a big deep sigh. It sounded like air coming out of a large deflating balloon.

I think I'm going to call James.

James was her therapist. We did a joint session, a couple's therapy session, every now and then when my wife felt overwhelmed.

He's going to see us for free? Or do you have some other kind of arrangement worked out with him.

I ducked just in time—the porcelain shattered against the wall behind me. Some of it broke during the crash landing on the wood floor. I left it there, got back in the car.

When I got to the bar of the club, I ordered a Manhattan with cherry juice. After preparing the drink, the bartender handed me back my secret credit card.

Declined, he said. Don't kill your wife, he said. Be easy on her.

I laughed good-naturedly. Ah, yes, I said. You can't trust them with these damn things.

I handed another, the one with both our names on the account. Fuck it, I said.

I had nothing to lose anymore.

I went looking again for Roland. I passed a benched man with a heaving chest. His breathing sounded like a man shouting from a great distance.

I met Jordan from Sacramento. He got off the bus looking for a Walmart but ended up here. He was barefoot and his feet were swollen. They looked like latex gloves filled with water.

On a set of stairs sat a woman with plastic bags on either side. She wore a hat, and on the brim of the hat was a piece of paper taped on it that said OUT OF OFFICE written in black Sharpie. She ate something creamy with the wrong end of the spoon.

I saw an almost full bag of blueberry bagels on a built-in table next to the docks. Seagulls tried to peck the plastic, but the bag was tied shut. There was a cluster of dew-like diamonds building inside the bag—they were going bad.

My stepfather was a sales rep. He carried a suitcase and kept a Rolodex. He was gone at the crack of dawn in his gray-flecked double-breasted suit. His visits were spread throughout the city, a never-ending newspaper route, he'd say.

My day was dependent on his day.

He'd come home with an ice cream Vienetta or a vendetta. I was the only child.

They'd tease me, my mother and stepfather, with the idea of a brother or sister, but one never came.

I started playing tennis when he took on more of a managerial role at the company. He made more money, and we joined the club as a family. I was nine then. I had taken a few lessons with a coach at a park. My tennis game accelerated after joining the club.

I started to compete at the age of ten—still plenty of time on the path to becoming a pro. A coach fed him that line, us that line, that I was destined for professional tennis. He told everyone he knew, and I called him my old man.

When the company went south, he had to find work elsewhere. I was fifteen. He became a sales rep again and dyed the gray out of his hair. He wore a simple suit with an open collar and he'd often come home empty-handed, zero greetings. My mother would retreat upstairs. She'd busy herself, and he didn't have much of an appetite. Instead, he poured some bitters into the bottom of a glass, filled it with ice. Then, he'd add the whiskey generously.

If I had a tournament that weekend, he'd print out the draw. Then he'd fill my name in the brackets all the way to the finals with an unsteady hand, sloppy handwriting. He'd write my name on the line above where it said "winner."

He brought me to my matches. When I lost, he wouldn't speak to me for days. He would tell everyone he knew, including members of the club, my coaches, that I had won the whole tournament. We would be at a restaurant, the grocery store, and he'd brag to them all. He wouldn't say anything to me directly, but I would have to listen. At night, I could hear my mother in the bedroom above mine protesting, but her complaints went ignored.

I headed east. Toppled purple shopping carts from the 99 Cent Store were typically a sign of vagrancy nearby.

I searched public parks. There was one near a train track that looked decrepit, abandoned, and promising. I found a dead rodent there in a patch of dirt and yellow grass. It still had fur and one leg remaining. The jawline was bone. It could have been a large squirrel. It could have been a racoon. The tail looked like a withered snake—hairless, dry, and curled at the end. On a picnic table there was a bee on its back, pedaling its legs in the air. I left it there.

There was another park squished in between houses, the size of two lots. There were shovels and rakes lying around, a hole in the fence. Behind it were railroad tracks. A sign read *No Dogs Allowed.*

At the 99 Cent Store, I spoke to Mimi. She said a young man comes in every day and helps himself to the refrigerated goods and leaves. I showed her the picture—Roland. No, she said, shaking her head. Outside, there was a guy on his back with his hands in his pants. I couldn't tell if he was scratching himself or jerking off.

At the Topsy-Turvy liquor store, I gave the owner, George, my number.

Above the business, on the hill, I saw a lone wooden chair next to a soccer field. It looked like a nice place to sit.

Another liquor store next to the Coin-Up Laundry hadn't seen him either, but at Royal Liquor, Joy, the owner, gave the picture a real long look.

Carlin's husband was a chiropractor—had his own practice, I found out. I thought of going to his office for an adjustment, revealing the news then, in-person. But I decided against it.

I had followed him home from his practice a week ago. I was behind tinted windows. I drove by as he got out of the car.

He was a handsome man with a Vandyke-style beard and a solid hairline of brown hair. He had a definitive Adam's apple but also a bit of a slouch for someone that should be a beacon of proper posture. Maybe he needed an adjustment.

Thiago needed an adjustment, too.

The fallout of this would give me the edge I needed during our future ladder match. I was banking on it.

I uploaded the photos from my phone to the website, and they were ready in an hour at CVS. I put the photos in a 7½" × 10½" manila envelope, sealed it shut with tape. Then, I drove to their home. It was night.

Their house was white with a brown garage, a small driveway. There were ring cameras, I knew, so I donned a blue ski mask.

The husband usually parked his black Lexus SUV outside of the garage, I had noticed, and when I parked down the block, it was there. I had handled the manila envelope, the 4″×6″ photographs with latex gloves. I wrote his first name in Sharpie—Edmund.

I set out on foot for his car, and when I got there, I lifted the windshield wiper. I heard the sound of an owl, the distant roar of a crashing wave, a dog bark. Then a motorcycle ripped through the evening coastal suburbia sounds. I let go of the windshield wiper, the windshield itself a little damp from the fog.

Let it play out, I thought. Let it play.

We'll see how Thiago plays after this.

I left the photos there. For Edmund—Carlin's husband.

They were photographs of Carlin and Thiago kissing. The other night at the bar. I took the photos with my phone when they weren't looking.

I had zoomed in on their faces. Their mouths were locked, smiling a little as they kissed, eyes shut.

When I got home, I deleted the photos from my phone.

I had Bray on the line with my left hand, and in my right I held the throat of the bottle—Maker's Mark. I was upstairs in my bedroom, almost noon.

I'll tell you what's going on, I said. I took a swig, felt the burn in my throat.

I got a call in five minutes. Don't waste my fuckin' time.

Look, I wanted to put you in singles the last match.

Bullshit.

I did.

Then why didn't you? You're the captain.

I took another swig. I set the bottle down on my nightstand. The blinds were shut, but some light was leaking in onto the mauve carpet.

Not anymore, I said.

What are you talking about?

Ken is backseat driving the team now. Someone complained.

Bray was silent. I heard him breathing.

You there?

Yeah, I'm here, I said.

Look, he said. A few of us complained.

Oh, is that right.

Yeah. Many of us. All of us.

Why couldn't you talk to me directly? Why couldn't you man up. I grabbed the bottle by the throat again.

You weren't listening.

Well, Ken is calling the lineups now, and I was obeying orders. He put you at doubles, not me.

Motherfucker, he said.

Yeah.

I felt the whiskey running through my insides like a racetrack. I felt warm, loose, like I could knock someone out—Ken, for example.

In fact, I lied, Ken wanted to sit you out completely, but I vouched for you. He told me he thinks you're 4.5, not 5.0. He thinks you're a liability. I fought for you, man.

You're fuckin' kidding me.

Nope.

Listen, I gotta go, okay?

You're not going to tell him, are you?

I'm gonna break his nose.

Really? Do it.

No, of course not. But you and I need to strategize before you release his lineup moving forward. Okay, sport?

And then Bray hung up.

I brought the bottle to my lips, took another chug. I shook off the aftertaste like a dog shedding water from its coat. I heard the faint calls of my son from downstairs.

Dad?

Dad, you there?

I held the railing to steady myself.

Coming, I said, from the top of the stairs.

I found my son there on the couch with the TV on. He was watching a video of young adults playing video games via split screen. He looked at me with concern.

You okay, Dad?

I realized I was still holding the bottle. I hid it behind the Hot Wheels racetrack on the ground.

Why don't you rest, Dad?

He patted the couch, the brown cushion.

I obeyed his orders, laying my head down next to him. I closed my eyes. The TV volume was lowered, and I felt his fingers run through my hair.

I asked for water. I asked for a snack. He brought me a cup. He brought me a bowl of popcorn, a paper towel. I sat up and sipped the water. I stuffed my mouth with the buttered popcorn.

Thank you, I said, lying back down. He ran his fingers through my hair again. It was midafternoon now, the sun lowering through the French blinds. I kept my eyes closed.

I love you, I said.

Love you, Dad, he said. I hope you feel better.

I could hear his soft voice still, and when I came-to, the house was dark, the room illuminated by the TV static. I was holding something, someone, I was cradling someone, and it was my son. My son was in my arms, his greasy hair under my nose, and he was asleep. I slipped my hands away and I pushed myself up. I lifted him and brought him to his bed up the stairs. I tucked him in, turned on the night light. I watched him from the doorway.

Then, I drove to the club.

I was scanning my key card when Ken called me into his office.

He looked a little red in the face. He shut the door behind us.

He pointed at the chair, and I took a seat.

Nice pink polo, Ken. Little early to discuss the lineup, isn't it.

He sat down across from me, leaned forward with his elbows on the desk.

You key my car?

What?

Did you key my car?

I don't even know what car you drive, I said. This wasn't true. He drove a metallic-blue 2003 Nissan Altima. Probably had 200,000 miles on it.

Someone keyed my car.

So I'm a suspect? Screw you, man, I said.

You're upset about our arrangement.

I weighed his words. I am, but I'm not the only one, I said.

How so?

I told Bray.

What do you mean you told Bray?

I told him you're calling the shots now. Isn't that the truth?

He sat back in his chair. I could see some perspiration begin to dawn on his forehead, a dampness, a sheen. He pushed his loose silver wristwatch, a cheap knockoff, to the base of his hand.

He was one of the complainers, wasn't he? I asked. So what's the problem?

I told them I would have a talk with you, not that I would feed you the lineup. That was supposed to be confidential.

Sounds like you overstepped, Ken. How would the top brass feel about that? I'm sure Bray knows them.

I let that hang in the air, scooted my chair back, hands on the arm rests.

You cause problems for me, I can return the favor, Ken. Remember, your position isn't permanent. You're a temporary hire, not a stakeholder.

I stood up.

Let me call the lineup for now on, got it?

I backed up to the door.

And I didn't key your car.

I closed the door behind me.

Two towels please, I said to the front desk. They clicked me in.

The fact is, I did key his car.

He had a chance at promotion, my old man. He felt a lot of pressure. He built me up, and his boss, in fact the boss above his boss, was obsessed with tennis.

I had a big match, a designated tournament at a fancy country club in another county where the boss of the boss lived, and so my old man invited him. He wanted to show me off, show him the next Ivan Lendl.

What made it worse was my opponent was the son of someone my old man played tennis with. The other father wasn't any good, but neither was my old man. They competed like hell though. They rarely said a word to each other in between games, sitting on opposite sides of the bench, both of their heads steaming.

This other man's son was a Peyton or a Paxton, I can't recall which. He was a pusher—he just kept the ball in high and deep and waited for me to miss.

When match day came, I knew this. I knew that I couldn't miss. I knew that my old man hated his life, his job, and viewed me as a way out. He viewed these matches as a way out, a fantasy, a dream.

I gagged in the morning in the toilet. Nothing came out. I had thrown the comforter off my bed in the middle of the night.

We left the house before my mother emerged. It would have been nice to see her face. It would have made me feel better.

My old man had his Thomas Guide, and he took us to the courts of a nearby high school in order to warm up. Lookin' sharp, he said after. Now, your second match is later today, this afternoon. So we'll just spend the whole day here, he said. I found a Subway nearby, he said, tapping his Thomas Guide. He looked like a confident man. He had placed his bets, and he liked the spread he was looking at. Eyes on the road, the radio off, he drove us to the tournament site at the country club.

I just wanted to make him happy. I just wanted to make him proud. I wanted him to place his hand and rest it against the back of my neck.

Looking back, I can't remember a time that he hugged me.

I knew that I couldn't miss. I could already feel my hand gripping the racquet hard like I was trying to save my own life.

Dear Ned,

We've received your email with attached photos.

We find your actions alarming, and we've notified the other captain.

Should we receive any further news of more troubling behavior, we will not only disqualify you and your entire team, but we will also involve the authorities.

For the record, the woman in question happens to be a family member of Maddock's, specifically his mother.

Joy from Royal Liquor said that she saw Roland. He came in for a pack of cigarettes and she had seen him later, when she closed the store, at the shopping center across the street.

I went to the furniture store in the shopping center, and they confirmed what Joy said—Roland had been there too, on a bench sleeping when they came to open up.

I spoke to Gustavo, a maintenance man painting a curb red. He referred me to the ladder at the side of the building with an 858 number written on it. He said to give that number a call. I called the number and then got a text with a new number to call. The new number requested a photo of Roland so I took a photo of the photo and texted it to the new number. The new number said they would text it to another number and then I got a call from a second number belonging to a security guard across the way at another shopping center. This second number apologized—*I haven't seen him. I saw someone like him but not him.*

There was a Goodwill nearby and the woman donating a Marilyn Monroe framed poster asked me if I was looking for something. I showed her a picture of my friend. She raised her hand to the sky as if pointing to a plane, but there was only a cloud. Then she adjusted the height of her hand, lowering it to the horizon in the distance where a smoke stack plumed a gray cloud into the otherwise clear sky—

There, she said. They are all over there.

The court was all blue, and the back wall was too. The lines of the court where as white as a smile—a smile I didn't trust. Peyton or Paxton and I were assigned center court. My old man had organized this for the vantage point. He had negotiated with the tournament director. He wanted to show me off. I already had trouble meeting his eyes at this point. He stood there like it would be a quick match. He didn't even take a seat. And his boss, the boss of the boss rather, was there too, in a blue suit like the court. Peyton or Paxton didn't even say hi to me. We were already enemies. I could tell he wanted to beat me—badly.

I won the toss and I elected to serve first, and the first point of the match I double-faulted, and I when I looked at my old man, he was holding his elbows, arms crossed, and I saw a look of concern flash across his face. His lips were set in a straight line and his jaw tensed. This was the first and last time I would look at him the rest of the match.

I headed in the direction that I was told. There were boarded-up buildings and camping tents. There was a pizza & donut shop. There were men idling around a liquor store. There were trailers, trucks, and vans lining the dirt roads. All the streets pointed toward the refinery.

Roland was nowhere. Roland was everywhere.

Before I knew it, I was walking to the net. Peyton—I remember his name now—shook my hand firmly, eagerly, the biggest win of his life, and went to report the score—his victory.

When I looked around, my old man was nowhere in sight.

I went to the bathroom first. I sat in a stall. I closed my eyes.

He was waiting for me in the car. I was nervous to sit next to him. The car was stuffy, hot. The air inside was dead. I had trouble breathing. He kept the radio off the whole ride home. He didn't say a word to me for the next three days straight.

He ignored me until I forced him not to.

At the foot of a street pole was a bouquet of flowers, and taped to the street pole itself was a heart. Someone had died there.

One gray building featured a single door without a lock or knob. How did one get in? Next to this door was a mural: a pair of praying hands and the words *God Bless Us All Pray for Peace.*

Another building had a mural of three crosses. Inside each cross rested a different message; *a good man, a sorry man, a bad man.* Which one was I?

My mother made a casserole dish for dinner—funeral potatoes, and we all sat there in silence.

My old man had his whiskey there. He never had his whiskey glass there. The whiskey didn't come out until after dinner most evenings when he was settled in the lazy chair, but this night was different.

My mother, she tried to make conversation, but my old man didn't respond. He just spooned the food into his mouth and chewed slowly. I could hear his teeth.

I thanked my mother for the food, and she *you're welcomed* me. This was the third night of silence.

There was a hole under the freeway, and I knew Roland was in there. I could smell him.

It wasn't your ordinary hole. There was a freeway underpass nearby and it wasn't that—no. The underpass had tents on either side that overflowed into the street itself.

This other hole was something else. It was only reachable by foot. It was a rat hole filled with tents and bodies. There was no light in there.

Cars raced above, horns blaring, semis screeching and rattling in the wind, and I could hear the voices. The hole seemed endless—I couldn't even see the other side.

I heard screams coming from inside. I stood there. I stared into the blackness. I called his name.

Then, I entered.

I stood above my old man at the table, his hands still holding his fork, his knife respectively, his head down, his face mid-chew. The words had already left my mouth. I stood above him—I didn't move.

His hands dropped the utensils. I stared at the clean cuffs of his blue plaid shirt. Then, he stood up and faced me. A crash then a sudden shatter of glass on the hardwood floor—a wall-mounted picture frame had fallen, and there was a throbbing at the back of my head. My old man had me pinned against the back wall.

He let go of one of my shoulders, his left hand spreading and then closing around my neck. I could feel my pulse as he held my neck tenderly, firmly. His amber eyes were wet.

Both of my hands held his, the one that held my neck. I didn't grip too hard either.

We held each other in this way until my mother got him to stop.

After that, we moved out of the house. My old man had a studio apartment, an old investment, that he put under my mother's name. He sold the house, kept the money, and married someone else.

I took my son to the overlook with a box full of donuts—regular glaze and chocolate, custard filled, lemon filled, strawberry filled and powdered, some sprinkles. There were a dozen of them.

I reached in the back and unbuckled him.

Here, I said, patting the passenger seat as he climbed through the opening above the center console. I gave him the donut box, let him take one—he took two.

Through the windshield, I looked at the skyline. We could see the bridge from here connecting one land to another, the glittering body of water in between. On that other side was a city. Skyscrapers, bell towers, tall and healthy palm trees. Some of the buildings caught light and winked at us in gold. My eyes were a little wet, giving everything an extra twinkle.

Why are we here, Dad? My son sat beside me now, in between licks.

I rubbed his head of hair, fine, like silk. I leaned over and buried my nose in it, took a big inhale.

Dad, you're messing me up. A glob of custard had landed on his dark green shorts. I cleaned it up for him with a brown paper napkin.

You've been a good son.

And you're a good dad.

Why are we here? my son said.

I was watching the buildings across the water, some lights coming on, others going off.

I've tried, I said.

Tried what?

I looked down at my son, his curious blue eyes studying me closely, not a blemish in them. There was a perimeter of glaze around his slightly open mouth. There was the small indentation to the left of his left eye—a scar since birth. I couldn't believe he was mine.

I've tried to be good, I said.

You are good, Dad.

I am not.

No one is perfect.

You're perfect, I said.

Next to us a car pulled up. I could hear the music, the deep bass and rumble, before the nose of the low racer slid into the spot. A young couple, windows down. The man in a blue Hawaiian shirt steering the car looked over at me, nodded, then rolled up the tinted windows. I could no longer see inside.

I had more to say. I was still holding onto something. I didn't know how to say it. I reached out to grab the closest hand, to hold it in mine, when I heard a rattle. A man in a denim jacket and a full black beard came into sight on the path beside the overlook wall. He was pushing a loud shopping cart over cracks and bumps with two full white trash bags in it. I could see clothes in there, the red lids of Tupperware, canned goods. He left his cart and came closer across the grass. He bent down a little so he was eye level with me.

Enjoy that sunset, he said.

It sounded like a threat, like there weren't many of those left.

Do you know that guy?

I turned on the car, raised the window.

Get in back, I said to my son.

We're going.

The night before our second-to-last match, I couldn't fall asleep. First, I tried sleeping next to my wife. Her back was to me, as she scrolled on her lit-up phone. I pulled out one of my earplugs.

What? I said.

Huh? she said.

You said something, I said.

I didn't say anything.

Well, did you want to talk?

Did you?

No, I said.

Neither do I, she said.

I went into my son's room and pulled out the trundle.

I left my son with my wife.

But I want to come, my son said.

No, I said. And he whimpered.

What's wrong, my wife said from the bedroom.

I didn't tell her where I was going. I carried my jug of pickle-juice water, my carton of pitted dates.

This is the most important match of your life. This right here? This is everything. I want you to do whatever is necessary to win this one. If you need to change the score, so be it. If you need to call a ball out that was in, I support it. Heckle them mid-point? Great strategy. Reach over the net from time to time? Love it. As your captain, I give you permission to do what is necessary. Remember there is no umpire or officiant here. We make our own rules.

What are those scratches on your arm from? Bray said.

Looks like you're still bleeding there, bud, Stout said.

I rubbed the blood. Didn't matter.

I'm fine, I said.

I left my men in the locker room for the gym. I needed to do some shoulder exercises.

I needed to use the foam roller. I needed to stretch.

Maddock was there with his men. There were five in total. There were only three of us.

I'm playing singles and I have one doubles team for you, I said.

So you're missing a line then.

I'm playing singles and I have one doubles team, I repeated.

Would have been nice to know that ahead of time.

You gonna go tell your mommy? I said. I'll be on the court waiting.

I kicked open the unlatched gate. I was on the court right below the bar, the balcony. I let down the Wilson bag, grabbed one of Roland's racquets. I held it there. The grip was a perfect fit. I sprinted to the other side of the court and did some grasshopper jumps. Maddock entered. I was playing Maddock. Good. He looked at me suspiciously.

I'm ready, I said. I don't need to warm up.

I grabbed a can of balls from my bag, cracked it open. I pocketed all three, then dropped the can and crushed it with my foot.

Let's start. Up or down?

I'd like to warm up first, Maddock said.

Fine, I said.

I fed him balls hard, side to side.

Can you maybe hit it to me?

He hit a ball down the middle, and I belted it for a winner.

You got a few screws missing, don't you, pal?

I rushed the net. What did you say? I said. I held my racquet in the air. I slammed it down on the net. Members were looking down at me.

You know what? Maddock said. I'm good. He walked to his bag.

So you're forfeiting?

Sure, he said.

I got close to him, and when I stuck out my hand to shake his, he flinched. He left my stuck-out hand unshaken and walked off the court.

I looked up at the crowd, and I raised my arms above my head.

I entered the steam room, towel around my waist.
Well I won the match, I said.
I said, Fair and square. That's a W. I'll take it, I said.
I waited. No one answered. I waited some more.
The voice—it was gone.

On my way out, Ken stopped me. He was gripping the door jamb to his open office.

I took a seat across from him.

So, your wife called, Ken said.

Wait, what? What did she want?

Ken circled something on his pad with a pen.

She had some questions, he said.

What kind of questions?

Look, Ned. I don't want to get involved.

Well, did she sound upset?

Upset? I think concerned might be a more fitting description.

Fine. She's concerned. I'll talk to her. That all?

We are all a little concerned, Ken said, looking at me directly. We think it is in everyone's best interest that we put a temporary hold on your membership.

A hold on the membership.

Yes.

Ken sat back in his seat, clammy as usual. His forehead looked moist. I could see some perspiration building.

Just go work it out with your wife, okay? She sounds like a very reasonable woman, Ken said.

There was a framed photo on one of the walls featuring the club pool. It was from decades ago. Women were in one-piece swimsuits and sunglasses. Some were reclined in chaise lounges, others drifting in the water on floats. Closest to the camera, a man sat on a diving board facing away from the pool, and a tall leggy woman in a red bathing suit towered over him talking.

The picture frame was crooked.

The man looked like he was about to fall.

My wife was waiting for me, alone. I got back to the house at dusk, and even though the sun was long gone, it looked like it could stay light for hours. I unlocked the door, the hanging exterior light already lit for me thoughtfully, and I went inside. The air smelled of scented candles—rosemary, sage, teakwood, sandalwood—and the dining room table was set, for two. There were small plates of salad, the heirloom tomatoes moist and glistening with balsamic and olive oil and lightly and sparingly textured with sprinkles of sea salt. On the main plates, there were filets of white fish, mashed potatoes, baby carrots. There was a bottle of white, its chilled perspiration visible. My wife, she emerged from the kitchen in a black dress with a slit, her face done up artfully and her hair let down naturally. She looked radiant. She looked proud.

Welcome home, she said, and came over to give me a kiss. She told me a shower wasn't necessary, to sit and eat, and I obeyed. I asked about our son—he was at her parents.

I know everything, she said. I don't blame you for anything. You needed this, for you. I understand. I've known all along, she said.

In between bites and sips, her reassuring words played for me.

In our dining room, after the berry cheesecake parfaits in glass goblets, I made us after-dinner cocktails.

You are a good man, she said, placing her hand between my legs.

We attended to each other devotedly.

When I came home at dusk, the house was dark, the house was empty. The outdoor light was off. There were no other cars in the driveway.

Then, I found a handwritten note by the key bowl on the entryway table.

Ned,

I don't know what to say. We are staying with my parents. Give us space, please. For the sake of our son.

I will contact you when I am ready to talk.

The note was unsigned, and I set it back down in its original place.

I went upstairs and found my duffel bag. I packed the necessities—shirts, underwear, shorts, pants, sweatshirts, a hat, an extra pair of tennis shoes, a bar of soap, a toothbrush and toothpaste, deodorant, a towel, a pillow. I grabbed my sleeping bag.

I looked back at the house.

The night before my match with Maddock, the night I couldn't sleep, I left the house. I drove to where I was going and I parked a block away. Then, I walked in the dark.

The backdoor was unlocked and I turned the knob. From down the hall, I could see the TV was on. I could hear SportsCenter, the screen of the TV emitting a full spectrum of light. My foot stepped on an empty can as I approached him there and he stirred a little, his shoulders shrugging, his chin turning, and then returning, mouth slack. He was asleep in his wheelchair.

I got behind him, hooked my arm around him—I could feel his slow breathing tickle the hair on my forearm—and then I got under his chin, and once I had him by the neck, his neck hair pressed against the crook of my elbow, I began to squeeze. As I tightened, he came to. On the TV there was a highlight reel of failed home sports videos. A dad sent a baseball through a wall. A son kicked a ball that hit a pan off the burner. Something caught fire. His fingers sought a grip on my arm, his long nails digging into my skin. I felt a sting and I wrenched back and squeezed harder until his fingers slipped away.

His arms went limp to his sides.

His body gave.

Laughter was coming from the announcers.

I sat down.

Dear Loraine,

I've gone to join the others.